SNOOZY SUZY
AND THE CURSE OF THE TWILIGHT PEOPLE

BY

BRIAN SANDERS

First Edition, 2022.

Cover Design by Cathryn Shahan & Elijah Stanfield.

ISBN: 978-0-578-39953-9 (paperback)

ISBN: 979-8-9869978-0-3 (ebook)

Library of Congress Control Number: 2022917469

For Julia and Alina

CHAPTER ONE

DREAMFFITI

Looking back on that strange, terrible, upside-down day when she joined a rebel gang and became the world's most wanted criminal, Suzy would always remember the blue lynx.

He instigated it all.

He and those Pajama Gangsters.

If Suzy had never met them, she could have stayed asleep. Her life would have been much easier and infinitely safer too. She never would have had to fight a beastly mare. She never would have had to plunge off a mountaintop with nothing to save her but a pillow. She would have gone on being Suzy Schuster, the shy, quiet, inconspicuous fifth grader, which isn't half as bad as being the world's most wanted criminal.

But, actually, if Suzy dwelled on it a bit more, she would be forced to admit that her thrilling new life began neither with the blue lynx nor with the Pajama Gang.

It all started with a dirty old shoe—one that, for the life of her, she could not find.

Suzy was late for school. Aunt Millie was shouting from downstairs, "Suzan, hurry up!" while Suzy (she *much* preferred to be called Suzy) was tearing apart her bedroom trying to locate it.

This shoe, like the one Suzy wore on her right foot, was shabby and beat-up, with faded laces and soles ground down to paper-thinness. They looked like something you'd see in a garbage dump or strung from a telephone wire. It wasn't as if Aunt Millie and Uncle Norman were stingy or cruel. Being respectable folks who abhorred standing out in a crowd, they were greatly embarrassed by their niece's ugly old shoes. They bought her pair after pair after pair, yet each remained in its box, never to be worn.

"Suzan Olivia Schuster!" trumpeted Aunt Millie from the bottom of the stairs. "This will be the second time this week you've been late. And when you're late, you make Braydon late!"

Braydon, Suzy's cousin, considered himself too old to be her friend. He was in seventh grade (she was in fifth), and he had pimples and some stubble on his chin and a voice that sounded like his father's. He teased her often, and though he felt bad about her parents, resented having another kid in his family's tiny, two-bedroom apartment.

"Snoozy Suzy!" he jeered, stomping into the room they regrettably shared. "You bedhead! Are you day-dreaming again?"

As we have established, Suzy was engaged in shoe hunting, not dream catching. But her older cousin's teasing got the better of her, mainly because it was true: Suzy *was* a daydreamer. She often spaced out in class and liked to laze in bed until noon on weekends, thinking and imagining. So, most everyone called her "Snoozy Suzy" and made fun of her.

"Yes," she answered dryly. "Behold my mystical dream sanctuary."

She was in the closet.

"I figured," he huffed. "Snoozy Suzy with her head in the clouds!"

Suzy exited the closet. "Did you hide it?" she asked him, gesturing to her feet, only one of which sported footwear. "Be honest."

"I wouldn't dream of touching your nasty shoes."

"So, you *do* dream?" Suzy smiled at him as she made for her bed. She got down on her hands and knees and looked. It was dark under the bed frame, very dark, so she stretched her arm as far as she could and groped around in the dust.

"Of course, I dream!" bragged Braydon. "I dream all the time. I have the most amazing dreams! Just last night, I dreamed I was on the moon. And I had this laser gun, and I was hunting my old man, only he wasn't my dad at all but a taco in a sombrero and…"

"That's not the kind of dreaming I mean," interrupted Suzy, extracting a pair of smelly underwear from beneath the bed—Braydon's underwear. She tossed them.

"And what do you dream about, oh, Snooze Master?"

"You wouldn't get it."

"Oh, yeah? Try me."

Rarely did anyone ask Suzy what she daydreamed about. In fact, it almost never happened. She climbed slowly to her feet and turned to him.

"What I dream about," and here she paused and shut her eyes, only for a moment, only to remember. "What I dream about is a world so beautiful. There's no pollution, none. Just blooming flowers and buzzing insects and air so sweet you can taste it on your tongue! In my dreams, President Finkel doesn't exist. And neither does the Unum or that awful monster that lives at sea. In my dreams, grownups frown less and smile more and aren't so rushed and panicky all the time." (From downstairs, Aunt Millie hollered again about being late). "And we kids have more time to play and make-believe and don't have to wear these yucky uniforms day after day. And, most of all, in my dreams, my mom and dad are still…still…"

Suzy was in tears now.

Braydon stared at her, slack-jawed and uncomprehending. "But," he began, "have you ever dreamed of hunting tacos with laser guns? Cause that's freakin' cool!"

Suzy boiled over. "It's not a nasty shoe!" she shouted and ran out of the room.

If Braydon had more sense, and a kinder heart, he might have refrained from ridiculing Suzy over her shoes. He might have recollected that they were a gift from Suzy's parents. Three years ago, just before they left on an important business trip, they gave her a brand-new pair of shoes, turquoise with white laces. And it was Mr. Schuster who had tousled her curly blonde hair and joked, "Who knows where they'll take you, eh, Goldilocks?"

Then Suzy's parents walked out the door and were never heard from again.

No, they were not secret agents. They were not special forces or undercover detectives. They were brainy professors, and I emphasize *brainy*—Timothy Schuster had his PhD in Psychology, while Olivia Schuster had hers in Neurology.

The police searched everywhere, then gave up. Uncle Norman and Aunt Millie consoled Suzy, saying that her parents would return eventually, then they, too, gave up. Friends gave up. Distant relations gave up. The funeral director was phoned and they had the whole black pageantry, which meant, officially, that everyone had given up.

Everyone except Suzy.

With Suzy downstairs, the Schuster family at last began their three-mile hike to school. Braydon, Norman, and Millie each raced along on two feet, while Suzy, not wishing to soil her sock, hopped on one.

They might have taken the train or bus, but there were few depots or bus stops in their neighborhood. Bikes were expensive, and cars were illegal for private use and had been ever since the whole Francis-RT9 affair. Francis-RT9 was a pig that escaped from a genetic research lab, stole a pickup truck, and crashed into fifty vehicles killing half a dozen people. After that, President Finkel swore to uphold The Universal Right to Safety (the only right left to the people) and swiftly signed a law that reduced annual automobile deaths to zero.

So, the Schusters walked. And as they tramped along in the brisk October morning, Norman and Millie in their office suits and Suzy and Braydon in their school uniforms (stiff black blazers with the emblem of the Unum—a blue dot inside a red circle—pinned to their lapels), the sun was rising over the city below.

New Shiny City, the capital of the Unum, was neither new nor shiny. Run-down tenement homes, fences with razor wires, plastic junk and garbage littering the sidewalks, filthy rivers spewing stenches into the nostrils of passersby—these were just some of the depressing, yet familiar, landmarks Suzy encountered on her way to school. But today, on this morning of all mornings, the morning that would change her life, Suzy encountered something unusual.

Down a side street, two boys were spray-painting a brick wall. They were members of that notorious gang of youths called the PG, or Pajama Gang, and Suzy knew this because they were wearing pajamas, though it was nine o'clock in the morning and they were out in public.

One, a tall boy with fair hair, wore white pajamas with vertical navy-blue stripes. A pillow was strapped to his back by means of a belt. The other boy, who was small and had dark messy hair and wore baby-blue pajamas with what appeared to be prints of red hermit crabs, likewise had a pillow belted to his waist.

In addition to their pajamas and pillows, each boy sported a kind of bandolier—a gold shoulder sash, onto which were pinned an assortment of colorful bags.

Neither boy looked particularly dangerous to Suzy. But according to the news, the Pajama Gangsters were wicked anarchists seeking to overthrow the Unum. Suzy, laying eyes on them now for the first time in her life, had to laugh. What, she wondered, does a powerful man like President Finkel have to fear in a bunch of kids!

In the next instant, Suzy heard the wail of a siren. Before she had time to process what was happening, a patrol car swerved to the curb, the doors flew open, and a pair of officers scrambled out and charged at the boys.

They were the police, officially titled Safety Enforcers but more commonly called Red Suits (on account of their crimson body armor). Their other cheerful features included combat boots and jet-black helmets with tinted face shields. The face shields hid their visages entirely and always made Suzy feel uncomfortable whenever she looked at them.

The motto of the Red Suits was "Safety By Any Means." And today's "means" consisted of black batons, which the officers shook threateningly at the youths. Suzy held her breath. The boys, however, didn't seem at all scared. With taunting laughs, they dashed down the sidewalk and darted around the corner of a building, while the Red Suits huffed after them.

"Roustabouts," scoffed Uncle Norman.

"Punks!" snarked Braydon.

"What they need," observed Millie, who was the most charitable of the three, "is to be put in reeducation camps. A little discipline would mend their ways."

These fashionable sentiments being expressed, they resumed their march. Suzy, however, lingered. She noticed something the family had overlooked—namely, that the smaller of the boys, in all the excitement with the police, had dropped his can of spray paint.

Suzy wandered closer, and closer, and closer. She picked up the can. There was a label on it that read "DREAMFFITI".

Suzy turned the can over and found directions on how to use the product. The directions were as follows:

1. Shake
2. Make
3. Wake!

Further down on the label appeared a safety warning:

"Caution: Dreamffiti is not intended to cure or treat any disease, except ignorance. Side effects may include mindfulness, critical thinking, heightened perception, and—in some cases— enlightenment. Consult your conscience before using."

"Weird," thought Suzy, but that was all she thought, for she was soon absorbed in contemplation of the graffiti or, rather, the Dreamffiti.

It was exceptionally pretty. A tranquil nature scene. There was a lush valley and pink cherry trees with bluebirds nestled in the branches. There were powdery clouds against a blue sky and a blue river flecked with lily pads and fringed by willow trees. It definitely didn't appear to be the work of anarchists who wanted to burn down the country.

"It's beautiful," she murmured to herself. "Like a dream…"

In fact, it reminded her specifically of her own dreams, of the perfect world she so often envisioned and hoped for.

As she stood there marveling at the art, the incredible happened.

It was uncanny, unbelievable, and entirely unexpected.

A white rowboat came gliding down the river.

It wasn't simply a detail of the painting Suzy had overlooked before; the boat was MOVING.

It entered from out of frame—out of wall, we should say—and coursed toward the foreground, growing larger and larger according to the law of perspective.

And in the boat, sitting erect on the bench and paddling the oars, was a person.

Or an animal.

Or, rather, a hybrid of the two.

It was a blue tiger—no, a blue leopard; no, a blue lynx with tall, tufted ears! Yes, that's it! And he wore a splendid bathrobe the color of tangerines or, if you please, a bright flame. And as he rowed, he sang in a deep, jovial voice this song:

> *Row, row, row your boat,*
> *Gently down the stream,*
> *Merrily, merrily, merrily, merrily,*
> *Life is but a dream!*

The boat drifted right past Suzy, so close she could smell the furry tenor. He smelled woody and sweet, like one of her mother's essential oils. Sandalwood, perhaps, with a hint of orange blossom.

Suzy was awed. Amazed. Thunderstruck.

She tried to speak but she couldn't. Nor could she bring herself to look away. She thought she was dreaming and in her head she told herself she was dreaming. Whereupon the blue lynx, as though he could hear her every thought, turned and winked his golden eye at her and exclaimed, "BINGO!"

CHAPTER TWO

TROUBLE WITH THE LAW

The lynx laughed heartily, and his laughter was like a warm ocean wave that plucks you up and carries you along. It almost tumbled Suzy over. She teetered and lost her balance, when someone caught her.

Suzy spun around and came face-to-face—that is, face-to-face-shield—with a pair of Red Suits.

She assumed they were the same two she had seen chasing the Pajama Gang members. This was only a guess, however. On account of their tinted helmets, they might have been another couple of Red Suits, and, really, what did it matter? A Red Suit was a Red Suit; she had never met one who was anything more.

"A little artist, are we?" jeered the first officer, who was male.

"Not at all, sir," replied Suzy.

"A little liar too," said the second officer, who was female, and pointed her club at the paint can Suzy was holding. "Have you lost your pajamas, sweetie?"

"Only my shoe," Suzy answered matter-of-factly.

"Don't talk back!" shouted the male officer.

"But I didn't paint it. Honest! I couldn't paint it if I wanted to. Look at it! Look at the boat, how it moves;

and that funny blue lynx rowing and singing and…" she turned here and glanced at the graffiti, but the boat was gone. The lynx was gone. The scene was static again. Nothing moved and no one sang.

The officers glanced at each other. "Blue…lynx?" said the male officer slowly. "Did you say blue lynx?"

Suzy regretted it at once. She had overshared and probably sounded crazy.

"She most certainly did," said the female officer and pressed a button on her helmet. There was a crackling radio noise, whereupon the officer shouted in a panic, "Dispatch! We got a Class 10 Offender here. Send reinforcements to 23 Margorp Street and tell the Commissioner! Over!"

Suzy felt the blood drain from her head. She had no idea what a "Class 10 Offender" was, but it sounded serious. If it weren't, why would they request backup on account of a dinky eleven-year-old?

The Red Suits stalked toward her. Suzy stood paralyzed, not knowing what to do. She might have run away, but she had been taught to always obey and trust the Safety Enforcers. Surely, they would be fair to her. Surely, they were only trying to protect her. Surely, everything would be okay…right?

Just then Suzy heard the nasally voice of Uncle Norman, followed by the squawky voice of Aunt Millie. "Suzan!" they cried in unison. "There you are!"

The Schusters bumbled over and glanced in confusion at the Red Suits. "Whatever is the matter, Officers?" asked Uncle Norman.

The Red Suits inquired if they knew the girl. Aunt and Uncle said yes, she was their niece, and they were on their way to school and were extremely late. The officers asked if Suzan was a member of the Pajama Gang, to which Norman and Millie laughed loudly and nervously. They emphatically denied that their niece was a criminal anarchist. She was obedient and patriotic. Why, she wasn't even wearing pajamas!

Suzy breathed a sigh of relief. For once in her life, she was grateful that her aunt and uncle were so utterly conventional. No one would ever suspect them of anything. The Red Suits backed off, though they never took their eyes off Suzy as she departed in the company of the respectable Schusters.

Suzy received a severe scolding the rest of the way. Even Braydon admonished her. At one point, Millie threatened to send her to a reeducation camp—her favorite solution to almost any bad behavior. By the time they got to school, Suzy felt miserable.

"If only I hadn't lost my shoe this morning," she thought. "I would've left on time and not been distracted by those punks and their graffiti, I mean, their…"

Dreamffiti!

She still had it—the can of paint. It was right there, clutched in her hand. Furtively, guiltily, she stuffed it in her backpack. Was it just paint? Or was there some strange magic in that aerosol can? Had she really seen the lynx and heard his song, or was she daydreaming again? It certainly didn't feel like a dream, yet there was no other explanation for it.

Everyone stared at Suzy when she entered the classroom. She was almost an hour late, which made her fair game for jokes and eye-rolls and protruding tongues.

"Snoozy Suzy overslept!" teased one boy. "Who would've thought!"

"Nice shoe," tittered a girl with pigtails. "Guess you couldn't afford the other one?"

"Anyone smell moldy cheese?" asked a redheaded meanie. "Oh, wait! That's just Suzy's sock!"

Suzy's teacher, Ms. Canary, overheard all this. But she was a shy lady and hadn't the courage to silence her students. She spoke in whispers and seemed fragile, like glass. She was allergic to the air pollution and therefore always wore a leather gas mask, which disturbed some of her pupils.

I should mention that not all of Suzy's classmates teased her. She did have a few friends. There were Fanny Ford and William Goodkind, but as Suzy glanced at their desks, she discovered that they were both home today. Probably sick. Suzy wished she were sick today too.

The school day, caring not for wishes, proceeded according to schedule. Ms. Canary pressed a key on her smart board and a presentation began.

Like all teachers, Ms. Canary taught nothing herself but relied instead on presentations from Finkel-approved scholars. Today's was from a wrinkly historian, who described the "olden days" before the Unum. Back then, he lectured, people could scarcely count to ten. They wore loincloths of leaves and feathers, raided their neighbors' property simply for the fun of it, worshiped peculiar gods, ate raw meat, drove fast cars, and believed the human body contained an invisible ghost named after the underside of one's foot ("the soul").

Every five minutes or so the historian apologized and beseeched the class to pardon the commercial break. Then commercials aired: a new toy, a new cartoon, a new health pill in the shape of a T-rex. The last was for the

Unum, and it ended with President Finkel, in close-up, proclaiming the slogan of his administration: "Many people, one dream!"

Almost in spite, Suzy drifted into her own dream. She stared at the wall (there were no windows in the classrooms; President Finkel had declared them a danger to children's attention spans and had them bricked over) and began to daydream. She dreamed about a fertile valley and a clear blue sky and a riverboat and a mysterious blue lynx…

An announcement boomed over the loudspeakers:

"Suzan Olivia Schuster, please report to Principal Winslow's office. I repeat, Suzan Olivia Schuster, please report to Principal Winslow's office *immediately.*"

Suzy felt her cheeks turn red as, once again, her classmates gawked at her. Ms. Canary pointed to the door. Suzy shouldered her backpack and left the room.

Why was she being summoned to the principal's office? Suzy guessed it was because she was late today. In that case, she might get off with a verbal warning. Still, in the back of her mind, she worried that it might have something to do with the Pajama Gang.

As she neared Principal Winslow's office, she modified her footsteps—slowing them and pivoting on her toes like a ballerina. Quietly, softly, she approached the open door of the office and peeked inside.

Principal Janet Winslow was a large, intimidating lady, who, earlier in her life, was the undefeated champion of a women's wrestling league. Her wrestling trophies lined the shelves of her office. We must congratulate her, of course. This afternoon, however, she did not appear so very big or intimidating. That's because there were half a dozen Red Suits looming over her desk. Among them was a tall gentleman in a black leather coat and a cap with a five-pointed star pinned to it. His nose was upturned, like a bat's. His ears were pointy, like a bat's. His eyes were dark and glassy, also like a bat's. To Suzy, he looked more humanoid than human, and this was, as we shall learn in time, an astute observation. He paced the office, cracking his black-gloved fingers, and every now and then hissed under his breath.

His name: Jeffrey Sikman.

His title: Police Commissioner of New Shiny City.

His mission: to hunt down every last member of the Pajama Gang and take them dead or alive.

"She'll be here soon, Commissioner Sikman," said Principal Winslow. She picked up a stress ball from her desk and crushed it in her fist. "May I ask what the child has done wrong? Suzan was always a little off, but not a troublemaker, certainly."

Commissioner Sikman fixed his dark, soulless eyes on the principal. Suzy swore she saw the ex-wrestling champion tremble.

"It is not your place to ask me anything, Ms. Winslow," he rasped. "But I will tell you this much: that girl is one of the most dangerous individuals in all the Unum."

Suzy couldn't believe what she just heard. It was impossible. It was a mistake. There was no way that she, the shy, quiet, inconspicuous Suzy Schuster, could be one of the most dangerous individuals in all the Unum!

Wasting no time, she crept away from the office. When she had covered about twenty steps, she broke into a full sprint. She dashed past lockers, past puzzled students and a few teachers, and hustled toward the main entrance at the front of the building. She was startled, however, to find a cluster of Red Suits gathered there. They spotted her at once and yelled for her to stop. But Suzy understood now that she was fighting for her life. She would not have obeyed them for anything in the world, not even her left shoe.

"The gymnasium!" thought Suzy, as she ran in the other direction. "There are exit doors there."

There were, indeed, exit doors in the gymnasium. Four of them. But, as Suzy soon discovered, Red Suits guarded each one.

Suzy felt despair. There were probably Red Suits blocking every exit in the school. What was she to do? She spun on her heels and, having nowhere else to turn, ducked inside the janitor's closet.

It was a small room that stunk of bleach. The lights were off, yet there was enough light streaming in from under the door for Suzy to see where she was going. She searched for a hiding place. There was a slop sink in the back. She wheeled the janitor's yellow mop bucket to the sink and crouched behind it.

Who could help her now?

Not her missing parents. Not her straightlaced aunt and uncle. Not anyone. She felt utterly alone, which in moments of crisis is the scariest feeling of all.

Her heart was beating fast. "This is like a bad dream," she sobbed aloud. It was the second time today that she suspected herself of dreaming, and this reflection spurred her to unzip her backpack and remove the can of Dreamffiti. She shook the can and aimed it at the drywall.

She had no idea what she was doing.

She had no clue what would happen.

She could no more explain why she was painting the janitor's closet than she could explain what happened to her parents or why she was "one of the most dangerous individuals in all the Unum." Much in her life made little sense…so, why not?

What happened next reminded Suzy of those coloring books that use water pens: with such books, you couldn't paint outside the lines even if you tried. The picture and its colors are predetermined. You just apply water and voila! That's exactly how it was with the Dreamffiti. Wherever Suzy pointed the can, a different color would appear. There were lots of blue and lots of orange. Slowly an image took form…

It was that lynx character again, in his saffron-orange bathrobe. He wasn't rowing this time but sitting among the river reeds, in a lotus position. He had a pan flute raised to his whiskered mouth and was playing a lullaby Suzy had often heard when she was a young child. Her mother would sing it to soothe her to sleep. Suzy remembered how beautifully her mother had sung and how warm and safe she had felt snuggled between her mother and father in bed.

"Now," said the blue lynx, lowering his bamboo pipes, "you are in the right state of mind. Fear fogs the brain and shackles the heart. Away with it, I say, away!"

Suzy no longer wondered at a talking, two-dimensional painting. She was so desperate for help, she immediately blurted out: "What'll I do? They have me trapped!"

"Only if you believe they do," he replied.

Muffled voices. Just outside the door. The lynx heard them and flicked his tail. Suzy heard them and flinched.

"We haven't much time," the lynx warned, "so focus on what I say."

Suzy nodded. She heard the doorknob jiggling, but she trusted the lynx and gave him her undivided attention.

"When you are having a nightmare," he went on, "you end it by waking. But you can't. None of you can. The next best thing, then, is to dream it away. To realize that you are in control. To be *lucid.* You have the power within you, Suzy. You need only close your eyes and believe it. Close your eyes, I say, and dream—it's your only chance now!"

The door creaked open. The lights flicked on. "Slippery girl," hissed Commissioner Sikman.

Suzy heard him clearly, and she heard his footsteps too. Yet she forced herself to shut her eyes. She remembered her mother's lullaby; she played the melody back in her head, and this made her feel tranquil and rather sleepy.

"That's it!" she heard the lynx cheer. "Now... *dream!*"

As the mop bucket was yanked away, as Commissioner Sikman stretched his black-gloved hand toward Suzy with a crooked, sharp-toothed smile, there came a roar.

Not a lion's roar, no, but the louder, deeper, angrier roar of the ocean.

The floor shook. The walls trembled. The sink split in two. Beads of water began to drip from a thousand points on the ceiling. And Sikman held his breath.

Suzy was dreaming of a great flood that would bear her far, far away, when a humongous wave crashed against her.

Instantly she was swallowed up. Buried in saltwater. Launched like a torpedo with the implacable tide!

The wave flung her out of the janitor's closet and propelled her through the hall, away from Commissioner Sikman and Principal Winslow and Ms. Canary and all her classmates. She spilled down the steps and out into the street. The great gushing current swept her along. Where was it taking her? Suzy hadn't a clue. Was that a shark fin? Suzy couldn't tell. In this moment the only thing she was certain of was this: she was free.

CHAPTER THREE

PILLOW FLIGHT

When we last left Suzy, a terrific flood was hurtling her to who-knows-where. Very soon she lost consciousness. And when she came to, she was soaking wet, tangled in seaweed, and lying face-down on something soft, pink, and spongy.

She stood up, plucked a starfish from her hair, and observed her vessel.

She thought she was on a boat, but really it was a giant pool floatie. An inflatable flamingo, to be precise, named Pinkie. It was the same one she had had as a child, right down to the masking tape on the flamingo's neck where her father had patched a small hole. When she was four, her parents took her to the public pool to learn how to swim and they gave her Pinkie to make her feel safe. Only now Pinkie had ballooned to the size of a luxury yacht.

Suzy looked around. It was twilight, and the moon was rising. In the distance she saw New Shiny City. And here Suzy was, a mile or so away, adrift in the city harbor.

The floodwater, Suzy realized, had carried her out to sea. And if the floodwater was not a dream, as she initially suspected, then neither was Pinkie or the blue lynx or the Dreamffiti or the incident with the Red Suits. It had all really happened. She was living the wackiest, scariest, most ludicrous day of her life!

Suzy glanced again at the great metropolis. There were its skyscrapers, there were its water towers, there its blinding billboards and cramped tenements. There were its veils of toxic smog, there were its plastic-strewn shores, and there The Statue of Safety—a colossal bronze monument that depicted President Finkel stepping on the ugly, fish-like head of the infamous sea monster called Nemesis.

Suzy had never seen Nemesis with her own two eyes. Few people in the Unum had. She only knew about the creature second-hand, from politicians and journalists and scientific experts (*Nemologists*, they called themselves). And what they taught about Nemesis boiled down to this: it was to be feared. It was the mother of all fears. According to Dr. Neil Spurelli, the leading Nemologist, it was *fear itself*—whatever that meant. It was what kept the people of the Unum afraid of the sea that surrounded their great nation. It was what kept them from ever leaving. It was said to be the deformed offspring of an anglerfish and a dragon. It was said to be impervious to spears and bullets and bombs. It was said to be so mammoth, it could swallow aircraft carriers like pills. President Finkel was always vowing to defeat it. But he never seemed to get around to it. The hunting expedition was always being postponed until next year and the year after and the year after.

Suzy hugged the flamingo's neck, fearful lest a wave overturn her vessel and dump her into the monster's mouth. She thought of Uncle Norman and Aunt Millie. She wished she were back in their apartment. It was boring there but safe. She wondered what they were doing right now. Maybe talking to the police? Maybe defending her? Maybe not? Probably they were glad to be rid of such a troublemaking girl. At any rate, Braydon would be pleased to have his bedroom back.

Several shapes flitted in silhouette across the moon, distracting Suzy from her musings.

Suzy thought they were geese and squinted for a sharper look. Then, from the sky, she heard voices— high, fluty, excitable voices.

Kids!

Suzy perked up like a marooned sailor who has descried a passing ship.

"Hello!" she cried, waving her arms. "Down here! Please help!"

With a whoosh, they descended: first a tall boy, then a short boy, and finally a girl. They had no parachutes, no ropes or ladders, and there was neither a plane nor a helicopter in the air above them. Their means of travel was, incredibly enough, pillows.

The girl and the tall boy stood upright on their pillows, riding them like surfboards. The small boy, on the other hand, rode his pillow like a bodyboard, belly-down, face-first, with a buckle harnessing him to it. He was biting his lip, the picture of discomfort, whereas the other two exuded poise and confidence.

As they neared Pinkie, Suzy realized why she had initially mistaken them for birds. For each of their pillows sported a pair of feathery wings.

They alighted on the floatie, the tall boy and the girl gracefully, the short boy skidding to a bumpy stop. As soon as they landed, the wings of their pillows folded up and retracted into the pillowcases.

The youths were wearing pajamas, and because of this Suzy automatically shrank away. Her whole life she had been conditioned to dread and despise the Pajama Gang. They were violent lawbreakers, she had been taught, who spread harmful ideas and endeavored to upset the peace of society.

The girl, who was more teenager than child and had beautiful dark skin and exotic sky-blue braids, was the first to speak. Dressed in a purple kimono and matching slippers, she turned to the tall boy and asked, "That's her, Orion? That's the one we came for?"

Suzy thought she sounded disappointed. A little bothered too.

Orion, who had buzzed sandy-blond hair and a wide, puckish grin, looked at Suzy and laughed. "A real Sleeping Beauty, huh, Sky? What say you, Hermit?"

Hermit evidently was the short, pudgy boy. He had big, expressive eyes with long eyelashes and a terrific mess of dark hair sticking every which way. His short-sleeved pajamas with their prints of hermit crabs rang a bell in Suzy's head. She suddenly recalled that she had seen him before. Both him and his taller pal in the striped pajamas.

"You two," Suzy said, "you were painting that wall this morning, weren't you?"

"Me and my bedmate Hermit were out fishing for guppies," explained Orion, "and instead we netted a whale! Not everyone can see Dreamffiti. Most are so braingrained, they don't even notice it. A few will see something: maybe a tree branch waving or a bird going flap-flap. But you not only saw Remmy, you dreamcasted that flood too!" He guffawed and slapped his knee. "You, a sleepwalker, a dumb drifter, a twilighted newbie! How prime is that!"

It was praise or it was mockery, Suzy could not decide. She could not understand half the words he used. "I didn't do anything," Suzy argued, "and I think I'd like to go home now. Could you please go and get help?"

Sky, the girl with the blue braids, clucked her tongue. "You mean, the Red Suits? Want us to go tell the Commissioner where you are too?"

Suzy was at a loss. In the back of her mind, she knew she could not return home, not with the Red Suits looking for her. And, yet, if the road back was barred, where did the road ahead lead?

"Nothing will make sense," Sky said, "until you become lucid. You still think Fakesville is Wakesville and Wakesville is Fakesville. But you'll learn." She looked Suzy over carefully, as though she were estimating her weight. "Or you won't. It's for Remulus to decide."

"Remulus?" Suzy wondered aloud.

But no one responded, for just then Hermit, the quiet one, the one who hadn't yet uttered a sound, cried out, "Trouble!"

Sky looked at Hermit. Orion looked at Hermit. Suzy looked at Hermit. And Hermit looked at the sea.

And where he looked, a craggy spike arose from the waves. It was ivory-colored and laden with barnacles and resembled an ancient pyramid both in shape and size. It was followed by another, then another, then another, a series of them stretching as far as the eye could see.

It was Nemesis. And, as the children observed, it was upon them.

"Time to up-and-away!" Sky cried out.

"I second that," said Orion, his voice quavering.

The three of them gathered their pillows and fluffed them. In the next instant wings popped out of the pillowcases. Sky and Orion jumped onto their pillows, whereas Hermit bellyflopped onto his and buckled himself in. The wings flapped, the pillows rose, and the kids were airborne.

"Take her," Sky ordered Orion. With that she yelled, "Excito!" and her pillow beat its wings and flew her fast away. Hermit followed after her, also crying, "Excito!"

It was now just Orion left with Suzy. Hovering a few feet above the inflatable flamingo, he offered her his hand and said, "Climb on, Sleeping Beauty."

Suzy glanced back at the monster. Waves rolled off its scaly hide. It looked like a sunken island surfacing from the abyss. Its enormous red eye (it had but one) blinked. Its jaws, atoning for its single eye, were many— mouths within mouths within mouths, all toothy and sharp and moaning in hunger. It drifted nearer.

Suzy turned to Orion and asked, "Where are you taking me?"

"Does it matter?" the boy crowed, throwing up his arms. "Your choice is to go down the slimy gullet of that thing or take my hand. Which is worse? I swear, you twilighted types drive me bonkers!"

"I don't like heights," Suzy demurred.

This was only partially true. While she did hate heights, she could still not bring herself to trust the Pajama Gang. They looked harmless enough, but didn't grown-ups insist that they were dangerous? Suzy's eyes were showing her one thing and her brain was thinking a very different thing. Which was right? Her education or her own two eyes? Why was it so difficult to see what was right in front of her?

Orion groaned, at the limit of his patience. "I didn't want to do this," he grumbled. He grabbed one of the small velvet bags pinned to his shoulder sash and ripped it off. He flicked open the green bag, thrust his hand inside, and flung a pinch of glittery sand at Suzy.

As the sand rained onto her, Suzy felt as if she would sneeze. However, she didn't because she couldn't. She had become suddenly paralyzed. With her mouth agape and eyes blankly staring and not a muscle astir in her body, she might have been a mannequin.

Then Orion, as though he were making off with a statue, picked her up and sat her in front of him on the pillow. He settled in behind her and tucked his arms around her waist. Suzy was still damp and briny from the floodwaters, but did Orion mind at a time like this? Not at all! He yelled "Excito!" and the pillow responded by flapping its wings and away they flew.

Pinkie, on the other hand, wasn't so lucky. The flamingo spilled bravely down the wide gaping jaws of Nemesis and was never seen again.

CHAPTER FOUR

MOUNT NIGHTLIGHT

If Suzy had been awake during her first ever pillow flight, instead of senseless like a plastic doll, she would have experienced many wonders.

She would have felt the wind blasting her face and blow-drying her flaxen bangs. She would have glimpsed many big cities, cities like hers, with ramshackle tenements and smokey factories. She would have observed Red Suits galore, many guarding the famous monuments of the Unum—pillars and domes and great gilded buildings.

Between some of these cities lay tracts of dying forestland. Highways crossed through them, but not much else. Perhaps they were where towns and small cities used to be, for here and there a forlorn grain silo or church steeple poked up from the canopy of leafless trees, like the ruins of a lost civilization. How many of these wastelands they flew over, we cannot say, for the author was not counting and nor were the kids. But in one of these deserted spaces there stood a mountain, and it was toward this that Orion and Suzy flew.

The mountain was not majestic. It wasn't even scenic. Its vegetation was as dismal as the land around it: yellow grasses and naked trees, many stunted and deformed. Brambly bushes, of these there were many. But no fruit did they bear, no berries, no sweetness. The animals that lingered here were few; there were mice with rotten teeth and bunnies with shabby hides and deer that limped and crows that laughed and robins that sang sad lamentations, lamentations for Nature. For She was in decline throughout the Unum, poisoned by a thousand things.

A misty rain was settling over the mountain as Orion made his descent. He set down on a shelf of limestone, about halfway up the mountain. Sky and Hermit were already there, their pillows tucked under their arms, awaiting Orion beside the mouth of a cave.

Sky greeted Orion with a glare. "You braingrained her?" she scolded.

"Ah, only a pinch," fessed Orion. "She was gettin' all twilighty on me."

Orion promptly atoned for his little trick. He unpinned a red bag from his sash, shook out a handful of red sand, and sprinkled it over Suzy's eyes. Among the Pajama Gang this sand was known as "red alert," and it was the antidote to braingrains.

Roused by the sand, Suzy sneezed and shook her head and looked around in a daze. Glancing over her shoulder, she beheld the vast height she had somehow attained. A gloomy wilderness sprawled below her and the city that was her home was nowhere to be seen.

"Where am I?" she choked out.

"Mount Nightlight," Sky answered, with a hint of pride. "A refuge of light in the endless night."

"Home sweet home!" cried Orion. He leaned toward Suzy and whispered, "It's not half as dingy as it looks. You'll see," and he hooted with laughter.

Hermit shuffled forward and nodded bashfully at Suzy. "My name's Pete Vargas, but everyone calls me Hermit."

Following Hermit's example, the others introduced themselves. Charlie O'Reilly was Orion and Trisha Weaver was Sky and Suzan Schuster was Suzy or sometimes Snoozy Suzy. Her nickname tickled Orion and Hermit, but Sky didn't break a smile. "Remulus is waiting," she said and hastened toward the cave.

A boy and a girl stood shoulder to shoulder before the cave entrance, keeping watch. They stood stiffly, with spines as straight as rulers. Like Sky, Orion, and Hermit, they wore pajamas and gold sashes hung with velvet bags. Unlike them, however, these two were blindfolded. No, not blindfolded. Suzy looked more closely. They wore sleep masks. White sleep masks.

"How strange," thought Suzy, "to blind your watchmen! How can they spy intruders if they can't see anything?" Nevertheless, as Sky and her friends approached the guards, the boy and the girl not only saluted but recognized them straightaway. "Hey, Sky!" they called in unison. "Hey, Orion and Hermit! Who's the newbie?"

"We're about to find out," was all Sky said as she strode inside the cave.

The cave wasn't merely dark, it was pitch-black. If Suzy raised her arms at her sides, she could have touched both walls of the cave. Besides being narrow and lightless, it was clammy and smelled of mud. None of these features consoled Suzy or put her at ease. Her feet, both the shoed one and the shoeless one, began to drag. She wondered what beasts lurked here. Bats? Bears? Tarantulas? More than this, she worried where the Pajama Gang was leading her. Maybe they were not terrible villains like everyone thought, but who was to say they were saints?

She was on the point of turning and fleeing, when someone clasped her hand. "It's okay," she heard Hermit whisper. "I was scared too when I first came here." He gave her hand a comforting squeeze. Suzy smiled at him in gratitude, only to realize he could not possibly see her smile in the dark.

"I smiled," she informed him.

"Me too," said Hermit.

They continued on.

They had covered perhaps a dozen steps more when Suzy discerned a prick of light in the distance. It was bluish-green and sparkly bright. As they neared it, Suzy saw there were more specks of lights just like it…they appeared along the walls and all over the roof of the cave. They were beautiful. They lit up the cave spectacularly and reminded Suzy of nightlights. Only instead of illuminating a hallway or bedroom, here they were, lighting a mountain cave.

What were these pretty aquamarine lights? Suzy was so curious to know that she knelt down to investigate one of them. Its intense glow made her squint. She reached out her hand toward it cautiously, expecting to feel heat, as she would with a hot bulb. Instead, it felt as cool as moonlight. So, fearing not that she would burn herself, Suzy grabbed it.

"Ooo!" a voice squeaked, wriggling in Suzy's hand.

The light was alive.

Suzy gasped and, falling back onto her bottom, released the luminous being. Its radiance dimmed as it fluttered its wings before Suzy's nose. Crossing her eyes, Suzy could just barely make out what it was.

It was a teeny tiny woman, with the pale green wings of a luna moth. The entirety of her thumb-sized body was haloed in moonlight. It was as if she were made of light beams. She had bug-like eyes and a crescent moon aglow upon her forehead and she was furry all over like a mouse.

Other of these winged creatures, having heard her startled cry, gathered about the tiny woman. They amassed together like schooling fish. By this means, they formed an enormous being—exactly like the tiny woman with the moth wings and big eyes, only ten times her size. And together, in a chorus of high, chirping voices, they sang:

> We are the Nyxies,
> Spirits of light,
> Shining pixies,
> Who sing in the night
>
> We are the farers,
> Of mankind's dreams,
> Secret sharers,
> Who foil mares' schemes

The Nyxies, for such these tiny people were, are proud beings and very fond of song, so that when they sing it is almost always about themselves. To be fair, they do play an important role in protecting our dreams from evil demons called mares. Whenever a mare trespasses into a human's dream, with the intent to frighten or corrupt him, it is the Nyxies who alert the Dream Guard. We will learn more about the Dream Guard later, but suffice it to say, the Nyxies are as useful as they are obnoxious.

"Pipe down, will ya!" cried Orion, waving his arms as though he would swat the Nyxies. "She's as new as goo and half asleep! Now, shoo! Get!"

Like fireflies, the Nyxies dispersed. One of them, however—the tiny woman—lingered. She hovered before Suzy's nose, her arms akimbo like a lecturing adult. "A lesson for you," she sang, her tinny voice straining with umbrage, "given with due: a Nyxie in hand is no firebrand, but a Nyxie in flight will grant you light."

Suzy quickly apologized – she really had meant no offense by grabbing her. Then Orion exhorted this Nyxie, whose name was Ulala and pronounced "Ooo-la-la," to light their way. Ulala fluttered down a dark tunnel, and the children rushed along after her until they came upon a rollercoaster.

Yes, there was a rollercoaster within the mountain.

It had numerous cars with seats and safety bars, and all of this machinery rested on a steel track. The coaster was painted azure-blue and bore the following decal:

The R.E.M. Express

Sky jumped into the foremost car; Orion hopped into the second car; and Hermit into the third from front. Then the three of them waved Suzy aboard. Suzy didn't especially like rollercoasters but, then again, she didn't want to be left alone in the cave.

No sooner had Suzy swung her lap bar into place than the coaster lurched off. It climbed the track, *clack! clack! clack!* It coiled up through the mountain lair, the track spiraling higher and higher. And at every corkscrew turn, there were those shimmering Nyxies dispelling the dark. Owing to their light, Suzy caught glimpses of paintings on the stone walls. These were not very sophisticated—they looked to Suzy as if young children had made them. There were flowers and smiley faces, peace signs and seagulls and stick-figure families, and there were messages too, like:

We R Lerning 2 Wake

Or...

Nekst Stop: Wakesvil

Or...

We Hart Remmy :-)

Suzy couldn't read any more of the messages, because just then the rollercoaster blasted off like a rocket. It accelerated without warning and shot straight up the mountain. The Nyxies streaked past Suzy in a blur of wondrous light. Suzy cringed and clutched the lap bar, sweating a cold sweat. She felt dizzy. Her stomach turned and her ears popped and her body shook, all of which served to remind her why she and rollercoasters never got along. She closed her eyes and waited for the ride to be over, which, thankfully, it soon was. The track abruptly levelled out and *The R.E.M. Express* hissed to a grinding halt.

It was dark again. Completely and utterly. The Nyxies were nowhere to be found, and Suzy had no idea where she was.

She called to Hermit. She called to Orion and Sky. She even called to Ulala. But no one answered.

Suzy shoved the safety bar away. She stumbled out of her car and hugged herself, less because she was cold than because she was afraid.

Before long, she heard someone faintly humming. "Hmm, Hmm, Hm-Hm-Hmm…"

It was the tune "Row, Row, Row Your Boat" again.

While the humming continued, Suzy perceived a pair of glowing embers in the darkness ahead. They were fiery and brilliant. They were yellow, they were orange, they were red, they were all the shades of the sunrise and had all its warmth and power.

Just then, a swarm of Nyxies whistled past her. They sped toward a rock ledge, some twenty feet above Suzy, and illumined a figure seated there. The Nyxies settled on the shoulders and arms and lap of this figure and by this revealed two things: one, that the embers were really eyes; and two, that these eyes belonged to the blue lynx in the orange bathrobe.

His humming trailed off. His furry legs and sandalled feet dangling over the ledge, he gazed down at Suzy with a wry smile.

"How was the trip?" he asked her. "Through water, through air, and up through a mountain—if that doesn't tire you, I say, nothing will!"

Suzy nodded. She had been so arrested by all that had transpired over the past 24 hours, she scarcely realized how exhausted she was. She suddenly craved her bed. She wanted to go home and slump onto her mattress and forget today had ever happened.

"May I ask," Suzy began, "why you've brought me here? I didn't do anything wrong, did I?"

"You were brought here, Suzy, for the chance to save yourself. Mount Nightlight is a refuge. It is where Lucids may live in peace, free from the pitfalls of the false world."

"What are Lucids?" she asked.

"They are the youth. They are the lightbearers, with eyes too bright to be blinded and minds too fresh to be tricked."

The lynx gathered himself up. He stretched his forepaws and arched his back and yawned, like a housecat rousing itself from a nap. This done, he rose to his full height.

"I believe an introduction is in order," he went on. "I am Remulus," and here he bowed, "of the Dream Guard. We are the friends of mankind. We are his protectors. We guard his dreams from the demon, Phantos, and his minions called mares. They, through one of your own, have put the entire world, the world as you once knew it, to sleep. Consequently, you and everyone else are stuck in the nightmare of one man. You know him as President Finkel, but Finkel is merely an illusion, a fabrication. His real name is Harold Dore."

Suzy nodded, pretending she understood, when really she couldn't make heads or tails of what he was saying.

Remulus read her mind, or else her expression, because he responded by saying, "All of this is not easy to believe, I know. Most people have no inkling that they're asleep. But you, Suzy, you have long suspected something was wrong. You dreamed of a beautiful world, not knowing that the beautiful world was true—was Reality."

Hearing this last part, Suzy was entranced. Somehow, the lynx knew her dreams and innermost thoughts. Moreover, he articulated everything she had always felt but had been unable to express.

Remulus licked his forearm—in a dignified manner familiar to all cats—and continued:

"I can show you the truth. But I cannot force it on you. If you wish, you can return to your slumbers—I'll have you escorted back to Aunt Millie and Uncle Norman's straightaway. There will be TV and video games to distract you and schoolwork to keep you busy. Eventually, you will become an adult. You will get a job. You will have precious little time to ponder and seek. In the private hours of the night, when you're relaxed and most yourself, you might question why things are so bleak. But you'll be groping for answers in the dark. And at daybreak, you will return to the false world none the wiser. There. I have said enough. Now, you must choose."

Remulus motioned at the ground. At the same time, several Nyxies detached from his shoulder and alighted brightly on this spot. Suzy drew near and discovered two outfits.

One was her school uniform, identical to the ugly black jacket and skirt she was wearing, only cleaner and dryer, with its brass buttons all shiny and polished and the pin of the Unum – the blue dot inside the red circle—staring up at her like an evil eye.

The other was a pair of pajamas and a bathrobe. They were easily the most attractive nightwear she had ever seen. The flannel pajamas were checkered red, white, green, and yellow and had a top and bottom. The bathrobe was a sumptuous scarlet and made of snuggly cotton. Resting on top of the robe, and matching its color, was a bow for her hair.

Suzy glanced back and forth from the uniform to the bedwear, from her old life to the new one being offered. With a determined nod, she made up her mind. She raised the red robe for Remulus to see.

"A fine bathrobe, I must say," said Remulus, beaming from canine to canine. Then, augmenting his voice, he shouted: "Lucids, please extend a warm welcome to our newest member: Snoozy Suzy!"

At this proclamation, a thousand Nyxies, Nyxies Suzy never suspected were there, lit up like fireworks and rocketed every which way in the air. They brightened the mountain chamber in dazzling shades of blue, green, turquoise, and violet. And by their light Suzy saw hundreds of kids. Youths of every shape and color. They sat in tiered rows, on benches carved from the stone and which gave the impression of a stadium. They must have been there the whole time, silently listening in the dark. But they were silent no more. At Remulus's urging, they cheered and hooted and whistled. They jumped up and down, as wild as kids can be, and chanted: *"Wake! Wake! Wake! Wake! Wake!"*

It goes without saying that every one of them was wearing pajamas.

CHAPTER FIVE

REMMY'S GROTTO

They called themselves Lucids, never the Pajama Gang. They considered "Pajama Gang" a putdown. They were not a "gang," they were a community; they were not violent, but peace-loving; and the only reason they wore pajamas was to remind themselves that they were in a dream. It was essential, according to Remulus, to never forget this truth.

The Lucids had all been recruited in the same fashion as Suzy, through Dreamfitti. Each one of these youths had been out walking one day, minding their own business, when—wham!—the graffiti on the wall sprang to life. Not every child saw Remulus; in fact, the vast majority did not. If a child were capable of seeing Remulus, it meant their *lucidity* was off the charts.

Lucidity, as any dictionary will tell you, refers to clarity of mind. But it also means being aware that you are dreaming while you are dreaming. In a lucid dream you will find that you can, to some degree, control the dream. You can fly if you wish. You can walk on water. You can visit that famous amusement park your parents refused to take you to. In short, you can be anywhere and do anything. The more lucid the child, the greater his ability to control the dream. That is why Commissioner Jeffrey Sikman—who, by the way, is 100% a mare—claimed Suzy was so dangerous. She had seen the blue lynx.

So, Dreamffiti is the first step in recruiting newcomers. The rest is accomplished by the Lucids themselves, who invite the dumbstruck children onto their pillows and fly them to Mount Nightlight.

After the ceremony known as The Choosing of the Pajamas, in which, as we have seen, Suzy chose a life of truth over a life of illusion, the Lucids threw her a wonderful party. The Lucids were as friendly as can be. They were infinitely kinder than Suzy's classmates at school. But let's not kid ourselves: they *were* kids, and as such they were loud, brash, crude, goofy, insensitive at times, impatient at others, and extremely eager to do everything all at once.

They had a feast that night, in that spacious mountain lair. There were fountains gushing smoothies, fruit juices, hot cocoa, and bubbly spring water. There were long wooden tables laden with roast meats, delicious salads, yummy tacos, and the Lucids' hands-down favorite food: pizza. Suzy searched for the ovens and inquired about the chefs, but she never found either. The food had appeared in a blink, and was nearly devoured in a blink too.

No party would be complete without music, and here Remulus, whom the Lucids affectionately called "Remmy," ably assisted. When the feasting was over, he appeared again on that high shelf of rock, this time wearing a bandanna and holding an electric guitar. Then Remmy, for lack of a better phrase, jammed out. The

Nyxies, circling the air, sang in accompaniment. There was even a drum-set beside Remmy, and Ulala divebombed into the snare over and over with her feet, creating a lively tempo perfect for dancing.

And that is exactly what the Lucids did: they danced until their legs couldn't support them anymore. Suzy, who was always a bit shy dancing, found the perfect partner in Orion. He had no shortage of dance moves, including one he invented called the Sleepwalk Shuffle (it involved covering your eyes with your palms while shuffle-dancing side to side). In the frenzy of the dance, Suzy lost track of time. It might have been morning, it might have been midnight—but that is what happens when you're having a blast.

Then Remulus, striking an awesome power-chord that rang through the mountain tunnels, bellowed, "Good night, my Lucids, good night! And may your light forever shine!"

With that, he leaped down on all fours and gave hugs to any who wished for one. Suzy held back and didn't open her arms. She told herself she didn't know him that well, and she never gave hugs to strangers. Yet she saw plain enough how beloved Remmy was among the Lucids. He was their friend, their parent, their role model, and, among the younger kids, their teddy bear.

Afterwards, the Lucids piled into the rollercoaster. They swooped down the track, the Nyxies shining all around them, and everyone, including Suzy, was all smiles and contentment.

The coaster conducted them into a long hall, whose rows and rows of bunkbeds signified that this was a sort of dormitory. The hall was cozy and warm, ideal for sleeping, though there were no fireplaces or heating vents to be seen. The floor was carpeted in turf—not the fake stuff, but real green grass, flecked with bluebells and pansies and home to many a musical cricket. The grass tickled the feet of the Lucids as they sprang from the coaster and raced to their beds.

Suzy, meanwhile, lingered behind. She was at a loss regarding where she would sleep. She figured she would have to share the lawn with the crickets and pretend she was camping, when someone called to her: "Hey, Sleeping Beauty! Over here!"

Orion, who had spoken and who shared a bunk with Hermit, gestured to the bed opposite theirs. Sky was already there, tucked into the upper bunk. She was not asleep. She had one eye open and was watching Suzy as she approached.

"Is it okay," Suzy asked, peering up at Sky, "if I sleep here?"

"Do you snore?"

"No."

"Sleepwalk?"

"No."

"Talk in your sleep?"

"No."

"Fine."

Sky rolled over on her mattress, and Suzy realized that she had passed the test and could bunk with the older girl. Yet, as Suzy was about to slide under the covers, she heard Sky again.

"Psst."

"Yeah?"

"It's your first night here, so I guess we should trade places." Sky didn't sound very happy about this, but within three seconds she was standing at Suzy's bedside and motioning her to get up. Suzy, not understanding why it mattered, clambered up the ladder to the upper berth.

Very soon Suzy discovered why Sky had offered to trade places. For as she rested her head against the pillow, Suzy saw that the ceiling was exquisitely painted. A starry sky, like that of a planetarium, covered the entirety of the domed vault. This alone would have been sufficient inducement to want to sleep on the top bunk, but there was more. As the Nyxies dimmed and the hall darkened, the painted ceiling came alive. The stars twinkled. The treetops swayed. Wispy clouds glided over the moon, while a shooting star evoked "oohs" and "ahs" from the children.

Then, lo and behold, a flock of sheep came soaring through the air! One by one the lambs arced the sky, and following them was their shepherd, Remulus. He was piloting a small propeller plane, with goggles strapped to his eyes. The aircraft's engine purred and the propellers buzzed. It was a pleasant sort of noise, like a lawnmower droning on a summer day. And as the good shepherd flew after his herd, he let out a jovial laugh.

Suzy smiled sleepily. And the last thing she said before her eyes closed was "Dreamffiti."

The next morning, while the Lucids were breakfasting in the reception hall, Remulus invited Suzy to walk with him. Ulula, who was something of the chiefess of the Nyxies, accompanied them, singing all the while.

They followed a slender rill through the tunnels, until they reached a dead end. The rill trickled under a curtain of stalactites and out the other side. The water was only about a foot deep and Suzy and Remulus were much too large to slip under those pointy stalactites.

Remulus reached into one of his bathrobe pockets and produced a blue bag.

"A little dreamsand, you will find, fixes most things. The Lucids call this one a 'shrinkle-sprinkle'."

He dumped some shrinkle-sprinkle onto his paw. The sand was as bright as blue sapphire and sparkled like ice crystals. Then, bending his back and coming eye-level with Suzy, Remmy sucked in his cheeks and blew!

The sand washed over Suzy—she blinked and twitched her nose and turned aside her head, coughing. When she looked back at Remmy, she instead beheld a huge furry foot in a huge leather sandal!

It was Remmy's foot, of course. Only it had become so ginormous, a family of five could have rented the space between his toes and lived there comfortably. Suzy tilted back her head. Remulus towered over her—a beanstalk giant, a Goliath, a Titan! At the same time, that thin little rill had become as wide as the Mississippi.

"ONE MOMENT," she heard Remmy thunder from what seemed the sky.

Dousing himself with shrinkle-sprinkle, Remmy shrank precisely as Suzy had.

"Now, then," he said, when he was as miniature as she, "let us continue."

He motioned to the river, to a gondola moored there. A gondolier waited beside it, holding a long oar. She had green wings and bulbous pupils and fuzzy skin that glowed like a glowworm. It was Ulala, only she was not tiny anymore; or, rather, Suzy and Remulus were not large anymore.

They got in and Ulala, perched upon the stern, steered them under the stalactites. They emerged unto a lake. It was, as Suzy reflected, probably only a puddle, but to their shrunken eyes, it was a lake.

The lake was surrounded by an exquisite forest. It was actually a flower garden, not a forest, but, again, perspective was everything. The flower stems were as solid as tree trunks. The sunflowers reached as high as sequoias. The roses were as stout as oaks. The tulips and magnolias and lotuses formed a jungle of vivid colors and sweet perfumes. At the other end of the lake appeared a lively falls, which graced the grotto with a fine mist and the most soothing white noise Suzy had ever heard.

Ulala laid her oar inside the hull and fluttered onto a Tigerlily, where she began to sing in praise of her paddling skills—an odd boast, unless you happen to be a gondolier. Suzy and Remulus, meanwhile, remained in the boat. They sat facing each other on separate benches. They rocked with the gentle current. For some minutes, neither spoke.

"I come here," said Remmy, breaking the silence, "when I need to shrink."

Suzy grinned. "You mean think?"

"No, I mean shrink. By becoming small, one remembers to appreciate the little things." Here, as if to illustrate Remmy's point, an emerald dragonfly with blue spots, which was not so very little compared to the shrunken boaters, skimmed past their vessel.

"Is this real?" Suzy asked in wonder.

Then, remembering what Remmy had already told her, she answered her own question, saying, "Of course, it isn't."

Smiling, Remmy dipped his forepaw in the lake. Suzy watched the water ripple outward from his touch.

"Today you begin your training," he told her. "I have every confidence you'll become lucid like the others— perhaps you will become something more than that," he added cryptically. "And every morning you and I will meet here, in my garden. And you may ask me one question, any question, but only one."

Suzy nodded.

"Now, then, do you have anything to ask me today?"

It wasn't a very important question, in the grand scheme of things, but she was burning to know: "Um, are you really a lynx?"

Ulula, who was eavesdropping from her flower (Nyxies love to secretly listen to others' conversations), chirped with laughter. Remulus frowned at her, then turned back to Suzy.

"Dream Guardians," he explained, "are spirits. In the higher realms, we have definite forms. But here, in the dreamworld, we may be whatever we wish. There's a story behind the lynx." He glanced at his reflection in the water. Suzy heard him sigh, but whether it was a sigh of gladness or grief she couldn't quite tell. "The first Lucid was a boy named Matthew. Later he nicknamed himself Quicksand, but I always called him Matthew. He was the first youth I ever rescued. He was an orphan. Remarkably lucid, but he had met with such mean characters throughout his young life, he refused to trust anyone.

"I first appeared to him as a man, but he ran from me. The next day I appeared to him as a woman, hoping that a motherly figure might put him at ease. But he fled from her too. On the third day I approached him as his peer, another boy, but he must have been bullied at the orphanage because he yelled at me to leave him alone.

On the fourth day I became a puppy, knowing not that a terrier had nipped him when he was small and instilled in him a lifelong fear of dogs.

"I tried other forms. A frog, a toucan, a peacock, a dolphin, a giant, an elf, I tried them all. None worked, and I was at a loss. Then one day I beheld him painting on a cave wall a curious cat. It was a lynx, with blue fur and tall, tufted ears. I later learned that the lynx was a stuffed animal he had had as a child. His mother and father had given it to him. It reminded him of happier times, before The Great Deception, when people were awake and wise and the world fair and bright. I shall never forget when Matthew first beheld me, in my present form. He bounded into my arms and refused to let go."

Suzy looked away from Remmy, hiding her sadness. The story of Matthew, you see, reminded her of another orphan—herself. She took a deep breath and tried her hardest not to cry. But the sight of her worn right shoe and her missing left shoe—the pair being, as you recall, the last gift her parents had ever given her—undid her effort at last, and she buried her face in her hands crying.

Remmy leaned forward and patted her shoulder.

"You will find them," he assured her, "you will be with them again. But only when you're ready, not before."

Suzy looked up at him, her brow all folded and furrowed. She was about to ask him what he meant, when she realized she had already used up her one question for the day. She made a mental note to ask him tomorrow morning.

But come the next day, she forgot.

She forgot all the rest of the week and all the next week too.

She would not remember this question for a long time. She would not remember it, indeed, until she was ready.

CHAPTER SIX

BECOMING LUCID

Every day at Mount Nightlight was a wonder to Suzy, and a challenge. She felt like a baby again. Everything took getting used to, starting with living in a magical mountain with 317 other kids (Suzy was the 318th member, which Remmy assured her was an important distinction, though he never explained why).

Truly, it would require something on the order of seven books to describe Suzy's training and all that she learned, which was considerable and never forced upon her. Lucids learned as they pleased and at their own pace. At Mount Nightlight there were no classrooms, no teachers, no subjects, and no grades. If a Lucid did not feel like participating in an event or activity, that was their decision, and no one guilted them about it.

Thankfully, Lucids almost always wanted to learn…they had come to love learning. Truth had value to them. It was the antidote to illusion, the repellent of mares, the dread of Phantos. It was what set Lucids apart from "sleepwalkers," these being the vast majority of the world's adult population, cookie-cutter people like Aunt Millie and Uncle Norman. Sleepwalkers never questioned, never spoke out, never risked so much as a hangnail to get at the truth. Truth, to them, was whatever President Finkel said. Lies were whatever contradicted what Finkel said. And the Big Lie, the Colossal Lie, the Lie of All Lies, that the dreamworld was true and real and all there was or ever would be, never penetrated their thick skulls.

During training exercises, Lucids of all ages and abilities joined in, from veterans like Sky to newbies like Suzy. The more experienced Lucids instructed the newest members and in doing so reinforced what they already knew. Remulus occasionally made an appearance but only to observe. He permitted the kids to guide each other and rarely intervened. Instead he would meet with the Lucids one-on-one, in the shrunken sanctuary of his grotto. There, reclined in his gondola (sometimes it was a canoe; sometimes, a raft or rowboat), he would ask them how they were progressing and so forth. He would listen very attentively to all they had to say. And he allowed them each one question.

On the first day of her training, Suzy was almost ready to give up. For the day's activity involved flying and Suzy, as we have already noted, feared heights. The rollercoaster was scary enough, but now they expected her to go tooling about the sky on a pillow.

In the bleary dawn they gathered upon Mount Nightlight's eastern face, Suzy and about two dozen Lucids. Amongst them was Sky, Orion, and Hermit. They carried with them flight pillows. At present, these resembled normal pillows, except for the buckle straps and the little flight patches. The patches signaled various achievements, such as "Falcon Speed," "Pillow Commander," or "Barrel-Roll Genius." In truth, they meant little; the Lucids could sew whatever patches they wanted onto their pillows and made up titles of distinction according to whim.

While the others lined up at the edge of the cliff, Suzy wavered irresolutely in the shadow of the cave.

"We're about 100 feet up," Orion called to her, from the precipice, "enough to make pancakes of us all!"

Sky chastised him. "Do you want her to fly or not?"

"Aw, Sky," grumbled Orion, "what's the fun of having a Sleeping Beauty around if you can't have some fun with her?"

Suzy was all nerves. She squeezed her pillow. Unbeknownst to her, the act of compressing or fluffing one's pillow is the trigger that summons forth the pillow's wings. And that's exactly what happened. Suzy screamed and released her flapping pillow, which proceeded to bob around like a lost bumblebee.

How the Lucids laughed! Even Sky laughed, if only to put the newbie in her proper place. Suzy, when she realized the pillow was not an evil harpy out to harm her, laughed too.

Orion leaped up and caught Suzy's pillow. He wagged his finger and scolded the runaway pillow, whereupon the swanlike wings drooped guiltily and withdrew inside the pillowcase. "You gotta show these pillows who's boss," Orion told Suzy, "or they'll never listen."

Returning the pillow to Suzy, Orion lifted into the air with Sky and the other Lucids, all of them shouting that funny word Suzy had overhead before: "Excito!"

Hermit alone hung back with Suzy.

"Why do we have to learn this?" Suzy complained to him. "I mean, what does flying have to do with lucidity or truth?" She stared at the kids zipping around on their flight pillows and felt the same way she did watching her schoolmates throw dodgeballs in gym class. She couldn't care less who won and resorted to daydreaming the moment she was out.

"The point of flying isn't flying," replied Hermit, brushing the hair from his eyes. He needed a haircut badly; Suzy wondered how he could see where he was going. "It's not even for getting around. The real point of flying, for us Lucids, is conquering fear. 'Cause if you're afraid, that means you believe in Fakesville. The dreamworld, I mean. And if you believe in Fakesville, that's how Phantos gets you."

"Have you ever met him—Phantos?"

Hermit's eyes ballooned. "Me?" he exclaimed. "I hope I never ever do!"

The boy's fear was palpable. He chewed his thumbnail and glanced over his shoulder, as though he dreaded Phantos might be there, lurking in the cave. Suzy thought it best to change the subject.

"There's one thing I don't get," said Suzy. "If this is Fakesville, then we couldn't possibly, you know, die." There was a long silence. "Right?"

Hermit shook his head. "The most hardest thing for Lucids," said Hermit who, being a few years younger than Suzy, didn't always use correct grammar, "is believing they can't die. None of us can do it, it's true. And that's why Remmy protects us. Anyway, when you die in Fakesville, you don't die. Not really. You're deep-sleeped is all."

Suzy wondered if the Lucids always spoke in riddles. "What's 'deep-sleeped'?" she asked him.

"Oh, that's like when you're sleeping but not dreaming. You don't even know you're alive. You're just...gone. That's deep sleep. OK, Snoozy, gotta go!"

Hermit tramped off. He buckled his pillow to his chest and flopped onto it, crying "Excito!", not unlike a cowboy hollering giddyap to his bronco. Then he launched upward and joined the others, who were doing relays around a cloud.

Suzy approached the edge and looked down—all the way down. At the base of the mountain lay a graveyard of wasted trees, their sharp, jutting branches more formidable than a bundle of spears.

Her legs wobbled. Her head felt dizzy. She considered quitting and trying again tomorrow. But what would that accomplish? Come tomorrow, she would find herself in the exact same predicament.

Suzy squeezed her pillow and dropped it hurriedly over the edge. The pillow did not fall far, for its wings were flapping hard. "Just a dream," Suzy told herself. "It's just a dream." She repeated these words several times. In this manner, she drummed up her courage. Then, closing her eyes, she lifted her right foot and stepped over the precipice.

Nothing awful happened.

So, she did the same with her left foot.

Again, nothing awful happened. Amazing! Although the pillow was soft and feathery and resting on mere molecules of air, it supported Suzy's weight without tipping or sinking.

She was doing it! She was aloft! She was flying!

Thrilled over her initial success, Suzy grew bold. She opened her eyes and peered down at the ground, as if to say to those gnarly trees, "Ha! You can't scare me!"

But the second she did so, her fear came boomeranging back at her. And the moment she became afraid was the moment she fell. She swooned off her pillow and plunged like a stone down the mountainside, flailing and screaming.

Had she met the ground at free-fall speed, Suzy certainly would have died in the dreamworld and entered what Hermit had called "deep sleep"—a kind of coma state. No longer would she have seen anything; no longer would she have heard or felt anything. In the real world she would still be alive, under the sleeping spell along with everyone else, but she would never have known it.

Now, Sky and the others expected Suzy to fall. They, too, had spilled off their pillows on their maiden flights. Thus, when Suzy plummeted, Sky was already swooping after her with every intention of catching her. But she never got the chance, and that's because Suzy suddenly remembered that this wasn't real. "I'm not afraid!" she cried aloud. At the utterance of those three magical words, she fell no more. Instead, she floated.

Sky drew up short on her pillow. Orion, Hermit, and the other Lucids also flew over. They were perhaps more stunned than Suzy, if that were possible. Suzy looked at them helplessly as she floated in the air, and they stared back in awe.

"Whoa!" the Lucids all cried. "Look! Look what she's doing! No pillow! No pillow at all!"

"But that ain't possible," began Orion, inclining his puzzled head to one side. "Or maybe it is…?"

Sky cut him off. "Remmy helped her," she asserted. "That's what happened. Remmy helped her, for sure." It was as if the older girl were trying to convince herself that this was true. She bit her lip and wrenched her hands and soared off in a huff.

Soon Suzy's pillow returned. It settled softly under her feet and Suzy was once again just like the others. This she was glad of, for she didn't wish to stand out or attract attention. The rest of the afternoon Orion stayed with Suzy and showed her how to maneuver her pillow (you steered them, as it turned out, with your thoughts and had only to think the direction you wished to go and the pillow would do the rest). Suzy didn't fall again that day.

At dinner in the reception hall, Suzy noticed not a few Lucids gawking at her and whispering. Suzy caught a few words; they were gossiping about how she had flown without a pillow. This, they found extraordinary. The next morning Suzy used up her one question with Remmy to learn why this was so.

"You will find," answered Remmy, "that Lucids rely on certain items to bend the dreamworld and do feats of wonder. We call it *dreambending* or, sometimes, *dreamcasting*. These items, like the sand or pillows, I myself gave them. Without them, the Lucids would struggle to dreambend. But yesterday, Suzy, you seemed to do just that—you flew without a pillow."

"I didn't mean to," she rejoined, apologetically.

"Just like the flood," observed Remmy.

He had left their sailboat (today their vessel was a sailboat) and was doing backstrokes in the lake. Every now and then he sucked in a mouthful of the cool crystal water and spat a fountain into the air. Ulala, meanwhile, was perched within the blossom of a nearby magnolia, where she sang stirring songs of her prowess with a sail.

"You didn't mean to flood your school either," Remmy went on. "Yet you did it, nonetheless. Spontaneously, you might say, like a reflex." He blew another

54

waterspout from his lips. "Now, imagine if you could dreambend on command...consciously, with all your will and focus behind it. What could you do then? What could you *not* do?"

Suzy left Remmy's grotto that morning with more questions than answers. This, she was beginning to learn, would become typical.

CHAPTER SEVEN

A HARD LESSON

Suzy's training continued with considerably less drama as on that first day.

Slowly a rhythm emerged: a new day, a new item, a new dreambending feat!

One day she learned about dreamsand and how each colored bag corresponded to a different kind of magic.

On another day she learned about wake masks. These were white and resembled sleep masks, only they did not blind one but, quite the opposite, enhanced one's sight. Wearing these masks, Lucids could spot mares from humans and humans from mares. That is why whoever stood guard at Mount Nightlight (the Lucids took turns serving as watchmen) had to wear wake masks. If someone approached, be he stranger or friend, those keeping watch could see straightaway if he was a mare in disguise. For mares, whose true forms resembled gargoyles, scaly and tailed and winged, were shape-shifters. Interestingly, the more depraved the mare, the harder it was for the demon to appear human, try what illusions he might. From this we may infer that Commissioner Sikman, who Suzy thought looked ugly and batlike, was very wicked, indeed.

On other days Suzy practiced Dreamffiti so that, on some future date, she might recruit twilighted newbies into their ranks. That future date depended on her proficiency with a flight pillow. At last, when she could race relays around the clouds with the rest of them, Remulus approved of her leaving on just such a mission and tapped Sky, Orion, and Hermit as her guides. This, he explained, was to be her final test before becoming officially a Lucid.

It was a cold, gray day in March when Suzy found herself back in her old neighborhood, which was called "The Downsized." To be back, after nearly five months away, felt strange to her. The neighborhood looked trashier and smelled fouler than it ever had. The air made her cough. The tenements made her sad. The police presence, a cop car on every block, made her nervous. The ubiquitous posters and billboards of President Finkel alongside the slogan "Many People, One Dream!" made her angry.

But the strangest thing of all, the thing that most amazed her, was how phony it all seemed now. Little clues hinting at the falseness of the world, details she had overlooked before when she was but a "dumb drifter" going through the clockwork motions of an uneventful existence, now jumped out at her. Wallflowers, when sniffed, gave no scent. The wind blew too regularly, at precise intervals of thirty seconds. The tenements were eerily uniform, right down to the peeling paint on the stoops. The soydogs and termiteburgers that a street vendor was selling looked, and probably tasted, like rubber. The sun, smoldering in a coal-clouded sky, seemed a lusterless imitation of the real thing. Everything was substandard; everything was cheap and artificial. It was as if Harold Dore, whose dream this was, had grown bored with worldbuilding and rushed his work simply to be done with it.

The sleepwalkers had something artificial about them as well. Suzy, dressed in her scarlet bathrobe and flannel jammies, with one very special shoe on her right foot and three woolen socks on her left, a pillow belted to her back and a few bags of dreamsand stuffed in her robe pockets, crouched behind a waste cart and studied them. She watched their movements. Stiffly and hurriedly they walked, just as Aunt Millie and Uncle Norman used to do. It was a stressful, scuttling pace, which permitted no idling, no mingling, no stopping and smelling of the roses. Suzy remembered it well and loathed it. For she had been a tortoise among hares.

The majority of the sleepwalkers held smart tablets or phones to their faces, said devices casting unwholesome bluish tints onto their retinas. They were probably reading the news, or playing a game, or watching a movie. And, yet, by a feat of peripheral vision, they avoided bumping into lampposts, little old ladies, and sundry other obstacles. They stepped around them automatically, like machines.

Suzy felt a nudge. It was Hermit tapping her arm; he was offering her a white mask. "Here," he said, "try."

Suzy knew about wake masks from her training. However, she had never worn one in the field. She trembled a little at the thought of seeing a mare for the first time. Yet, just like flying, she would have to stomach her fears and derive courage from what Remmy called "the Big Truth": that this world was but a passing dream, and therefore there was nothing to fear. Mares could trick you. They could scare you. They could even deep-sleep you, which was the greatest trick of all, to fool you into thinking you were dead. But the truth of it was they could harm you no more than the shadows on your bedroom wall.

Suzy slipped on the mask. She could still see, of course. Despite having cotton clasped to her eye sockets, she could see as well as before. She stared at the sleepwalkers streaming past her. They were human, all of them. This encouraged her. If they were human, they could be awakened. If they could be awakened, they could be saved.

"If you see a mare," Sky instructed her, "shout 'Beware!' Alright, team, move out!"

From their redoubt behind the waste cart the three Lucids and their trainee dashed to a city bus parked across the street. There were no passengers on the bus. It was out-of-service while the driver was grabbing lunch at a nearby café called Unum Bites.

Lucids loved to spray-paint buses because, as Orion explained, "It's advertising on wheels! Just think of all the kids that'll see it!"

They got to work, all four of them spraying with glee. Within ten minutes, the entire length of the bus was illustrated. It was a quaint prairie scene, with a cloudless sky and a lemon-yellow sun and a red farmhouse and a whirring windmill and a bullpen with bulls milling here and there and, for those who could see him, a grinning blue lynx in a cowboy hat and boots, riding a stallion barebacked and twirling his lasso in the air with a shout of, "Round up the Lucids, yeee-haaaaw, round up the lightbearers, wooo-eeee!"

While they were painting, a handful of sleepwalkers (not as many as you might expect, owing to their zombie-like focus on their devices) spied them. They immediately phoned the police using said devices. Far from intimidating Suzy and the others, however, this only made their escape more exhilarating. For it was, as Suzy discovered, thrilling not merely to break the law, but to do so in the service of a noble cause. They ran away giggling before the Red Suits arrived.

As they were fleeing, Suzy's eye strayed for a split second and glanced through the grimy window of Unum Bites.

Suzy dug in her heels.

She held her breath and looked again to be sure.

It was Uncle Norman.

Uncle Norman with his receding hairline and strangulating necktie and mole-like squint, as though the tax office where he worked were a fathomless hole in the earth.

Opposite him at the table sat Aunt Millie.

Aunt Millie with her floral dress and girlish orange pigtails and overdone makeup and prim, A-student rectitude, which led her to become a Censor Tech for Finkelnet, the largest and only search engine in the Unum.

They were a pathetic twosome, to be sure. Even Suzy at the age of eleven sensed this. But they were not mares—Suzy, who was wearing the wake mask, was relieved to see this. Moreover, they were family and she still loved them, flaws and all. Was it not her duty, therefore, to help them—to open their eyes to the true state of the world and the forces of evil that oppressed them?

She opened the door to Unum Bites and went inside.

Orion, Hermit, and Sky, meanwhile, did not realize that they were down a member. They kept to their heels and very soon ascended on their pillows.

There were bells on the glass door, and when Suzy entered they jingled as though to announce her to the patrons. Almost everyone turned to look at her. One man spat up his coffee. A little girl ducked behind her chair. A party of middle-aged women hurriedly rose from their table and left. Suzy, hoping to make herself more agreeable in appearance, lifted her wake mask onto her forehead.

The greeter, a teenager with braces and a certain pugnacious look, grimaced at Suzy. She pointed her pink fingernail to a laminated sign taped to her rostrum, which read: "Pajama Gang NOT served here."

"In case you can't read," said the greeter, "we don't serve your kind. Now scram before I call the Safety Enforcers. You hear me, girl? I said beat it or I'll—hey, what's that?"

It was a green velvet bag, and with a pinch of its contents Suzy silenced her. Braingrained, the teenager wasn't half as ornery. She just stared off into space while a glob of drool oozed down her chin. Suzy brushed past her and continued to her aunt and uncle's table.

They were slurping cold corn soup, topped with salted crickets. They shoveled the crunchy yellow gruel into their mouths without relish, both of them absorbed in their devices. Aunt Millie was scrolling through the headlines on her tablet. Uncle Norman was watching a movie via his smart glasses.

"Hello," said Suzy, rather shyly.

"Can we get a refill of water?" asked Uncle Norman. Then, in an outburst of violence, which he never expressed except when watching movies, he erupted: "What are you waiting for? Shoot him already! Shoot him!"

"And I'd like a coffee," said Aunt Millie, without looking up, "to go, please."

"It's me," said Suzy. "Suzan."

Slowly, Uncle Norman removed his glasses. Slowly, Aunt Millie looked up. They gazed upon Suzy as if she were a ghost. For that is what they thought she was. Owing to the false report of Commissioner Sikman, they had accepted that their poor Suzan had died in a freak accident at school—a water main had burst, there was a flood, Suzy was swept away, and, well, it was all very sad and tragic. Now, five months later, here she was again—only, she was not blue or waterlogged. She wasn't even damp! She was dry and, more, glowed with health.

But what in the name of Nemesis was she wearing?!

A...bathrobe?

And...pajamas?

How vulgar! How obscene! How criminal!

Uncle Norman recoiled, and Aunt Millie, who was easily scared, tipped backwards in her chair.

Suzy went to help her up, but Aunt Millie squealed and shook like a frightened pig when Suzy touched her. Uncle Norman, recovering his senses, bent his knee like a knight of yore to raise her up. "Pajama Gang," muttered Aunt Millie, all sweaty and cross-eyed, "she's a PG, Norm, a PG!"

"Darling," he began, his voice quivering with pathos, "I am quite sure it's a mistake." He turned to Suzy. "Tell her, Suzan. Tell her it's a mistake. An innocent mistake. You forgot to change this morning, yes? You were in such a hurry to see us, you plum forgot to change out of your jammies. That's what happened, isn't it?"

He clung to this explanation as a snail clings to a rock amidst a Category 5 hurricane.

Suzy faltered for words.

"Um, well, uh, not exactly. You see, Uncle, I'm becoming lucid."

"There you have it," concluded Uncle Norman, fanning Aunt Millie's face with her tablet. "She's only becoming lucid. Just a little lucid, that's all. Nothing to fret about it."

He had no idea what he was babbling about, but his focus was on Aunt Millie and Aunt Millie's focus was on the patrons of the restaurant who were gawking at her and, no doubt, judging her. It was her worst nightmare to be deemed disrespectable by the respectable crowd.

Suzy continued. "I'm happy there with the other children. There is a spirit, a Dream Guardian, that looks after us. His name is Remulus, or Remmy for short. He's a blue lynx, only that's not his real form…"

The more she spoke, the paler Aunt Millie became. It was as if Suzy's words were slowly choking her.

"Remmy taught me that the world—this world—isn't real. It's a dream, a bad dream. All of us," said Suzy, raising her voice and gazing round at the other diners, "all of us need to wake up or else we'll never be free! We're controlled by fear; we're trapped in an illusion! This table isn't real," and she struck the table with her fist, "this chair isn't real," and she struck the chair with her foot, "and President Finkel isn't real either!"

At this, Aunt Millie let out an agonized moan and fainted. Uncle Norman, on his knees, cradling his limp wife, turned furiously upon Suzy. His small molish eyes squinted more intensely than ever before…they were hardly eyes, just slits. "Look what you've done!" he fumed. "You turn up in pa-pa-pa—" he could not bring himself to say the word, "and then you go and insult Finkel! Finkel, our leader, our president, our duly elected chief executive!" It was the criticism of Finkel, you see, that most upset Uncle Norman. The stuff about the dreamworld and the unreality of things flew right over his balding head.

"It's all true, though!" Suzy protested. "And I'll prove it—see!"

She fished in her pocket for a certain velvet bag. The bag was yellow, which meant it was grandsand. Grandsand has the opposite effect of blue sand, AKA shrinkle-sprinkle. She dumped the yellow grandsand over her head. In a second or two, she was as tall as Uncle Norman.

Now, had Suzy been more careful and less caught up in the moment, she might have measured out a judicious amount of grandsand and dosed herself accordingly. As it were, she had given herself something of a sand shower. Thus, after attaining the height of Uncle Norman, she did not stop there but kept enlarging. Soon, the red bow in her hair was scraping against the tin ceiling! To fit inside the restaurant, she had to hunch over, now bend at the waist, now sit on her bottom. She looked like a lioness crammed inside a kitten's cage. The patrons ran screaming. The staff ran screaming. Uncle Norman picked up Aunt Millie and ran screaming. Even the greeter, rousted from her drooling stupor by all the commotion, ran screaming.

"Oh, no!" cried Suzy as she kept growing and growing.

To relieve the uncomfortable contortion of her cramped limbs, Suzy stuck her right leg out the door. If you had walked past Unum Bites, just then, you would have witnessed a most singular sight: a humongous shoe, protruding from the doorway up to the ankle. Her left leg shot in the opposite direction, into the kitchen, where her foot met something fiercely hot. Indeed, her foot had landed upon a stove. Her outer sock caught fire (it was a good thing she was wearing three of them). Suzy yelped and like a raging elephant bailed from the eatery. She smashed through the façade and in an explosion of rubble, plaster, tin, and woodchips swerved into the street. She plunged her heel into a pothole brimming with muddy rainwater and sighed in relief.

This relief proved short-lived. For, just then, an icy voice—a voice that could freeze the blood in all three of your heart's major arteries—penetrated her elephantine ears.

"Suzan Schuster!" cried the voice.

It was Commissioner Jeffrey Sikman. He stood at the vanguard of a company of Red Suits. In their crimson body armor and tinted helmet shields, they huddled beside their siren-flashing squad cars with guns and tasers at the ready.

Suzy suspected by now that Sikman's human appearance was a coverup, a costume, a lie. Dropping the wake mask over her eyes was almost unnecessary, and yet she wanted to behold him as he truly was—if only to convince herself that she wasn't crazy. So, availing herself of the mask, she looked at Sikman the man and saw Sikman the monster: a hideous horned batlike creature, with dark brown fur and a sweeping tail! A pair of leathery wings hung from his back. His feet were cloven. His teeth, like nails. He was a mere fraction of Suzy's current height, but it made no difference: he was terrifying.

"*Mare*," Suzy murmured to herself.

Sikman overheard her and bristled. He glanced behind him at his subordinates, quickly, furtively, and it occurred to Suzy that the Safety Enforcers probably had no idea that the man they served was a demon.

"Afraid are we?" taunted Sikman, twisting back around. He didn't wait for Suzy to answer. "You ought to be. Safety Enforcers…*grab her!*"

As the Red Suits charged at her like an army of fire-ants, Suzy turned and bolted. She squeezed herself into an alley between Unum Bites and a pawn shop. A rusty fire escape sprawled up the side of the latter building, and Suzy grabbed hold of the railing on the second floor and pulled herself up. The Red Suits fired on her—little electrified darts, which to the oversized girl felt as benign as the shocks one receives from plastic slides. Others climbed after her using harnesses and ropes. But they could not keep pace with Suzy, who, clambering like a giant ape, reached the roof in no time.

Suzy leaned wearily against a water tower. She had caught perhaps a single breath, when a figure dove at her from the clouds.

"Snoozy!" shouted Sky, riding her pillow like a hoverboard. She was piping mad, and her mouth was pursed tight. "Have you lost your mind?! We were looking all over for you!"

"I'm sorry!" Suzy lamented.

"Don't be sorry, be smart! Shrinkle-sprinkle yourself and let's up-and-away!"

Suzy did as the older girl bade her. She shrank to her accustomed height, fluffed her pillow, and took off after Sky.

Suzy felt terrible that she had almost been caught. She felt badly that she had scared her friends and darted off without telling them. She felt she had failed Remmy most of all.

Yet, upon her return to the mountain, he was rather gentle on her, and merely said it was worth neither the effort nor the risk trying to enlighten your average sleepwalker. To make his point, he showed her an evening newspaper from that day (how he procured it, Suzy had no idea, but Remmy was full of magical secrets).

Suzy's photo—it was her government photo ID, which she hated because her eyes were closed in it—accompanied the article. The headline in bold, capitalized letters read: "**ALERT: DANGER: CODE RED!!!**" The article's subheading, only slightly less hysterical, ran: "Crazy PG Member Attacks Diners!"

Suzy scanned the rest of the article, which was almost a page long. The gist of it was this: although some fifty people had witnessed an ordinary girl grow as tall as a giraffe, it was nonetheless untrue. The article referenced Unum's leading scientists, their consensus being that the incredible growth spurt was a forgery. The scientists went to great lengths explaining how such an illusion could be accomplished, using, for instance, dry ice and a projector or by arranging one's environment to distort perspective. One scientist, a pharmacologist, maintained that Suzy had drugged everyone's drinks at the restaurant and produced a mass hallucination. In short, the giant was a hoax and the girl, an enemy of the state. But the icing on the cake was a quote from none other than Uncle Norman, which went: "Never did I imagine my niece capable of slandering our President!"

He was still stuck on that.

Suzy handed the newspaper back to Remmy, too stunned for words. She went to bed early that night, with much on her mind. For she had learned a hard lesson that day: that the twilight people saw not with their own eyes, nor thought with their own brains, but saw and thought and lived at the direction of the Unum.

Chapter Eight

The Lighting Ceremony

After her debacle at the restaurant, Suzy was ready to wash her hands of Fakesville once and for all.

Remmy was right, as usual. It was futile trying to enlighten sleepwalkers. When you did try, they got all hot and bothered. Rather than engage in free thinking and open debate, they outsourced their beliefs to experts, pundits, and authority figures—all subservient, in one way or another, to Finkel's regime. People were taught that the Unum was universally good; they were conditioned to love Finkel like a father; they were indoctrinated to obey and serve and never question. What could the Pajama Gang's message be, therefore, but a pack of nasty lies?

So, yes, Suzy was done with Fakesville, at least for the time being. She didn't miss it at all. Life at Mount Nightlight was much more fun anyway; the food tasted better, the kids were nicer, and there was always something new to learn.

Soon the day arrived when Suzy was to be *lighted*. When Remulus lighted you, you were officially made a Lucid. You received a Diploma of Lucidity, along with the gold sash of the order. It was a quieter affair than The Choosing of the Pajamas, less a rocking party than a solemn rite. Accordingly, it began before sunup, with Remmy beating a gong and rousing the groggy Lucids from their bunks. After a tasty pancake breakfast, during which Suzy sat at the head table beside Remmy while the Lucids took turns relating anecdotes about her, whether kind or praising or just plain funny, the Lucids lit wax candles and gathered on the stone benches of the reception hall. Suzy, meanwhile, followed Remmy to his high altar of rock. At his beckoning, she knelt before him. Remmy then recited The Sacred Oath of the Lucid and asked Suzy if she "swore always to resist fear and uphold truth, to stand up to evil and protect her fellow Lucids as they protected her?"

In a small but steely voice, Suzy said, "I do."

Remmy draped the gold sash over her shoulder. Ulala appeared just then, her wings humming like a bee's, and held out a jar to Remmy. The glass jar, no bigger than a small vial, was stuffed with sand. Remmy took it and pulled out the stopper and poured the sand onto his paw. Suzy had never seen such sand before…it was white and shimmering, like crushed diamond. But it wasn't merely shimmering, it was giving off its own light.

"Sand of sunrise," declared Remmy, "sand of the aurora, sand of dawn light frozen in matter."

As part of the ritual, he smeared the brilliant white sand onto Suzy's forehead—Suzy didn't know it, but it was right where her third eye or pineal gland was located. Soon her head, or rather the sand on her head, began to glow. Subtly at first, but then brighter and brighter until she could barely see in front of her.

At the same time that she was losing her sight, she was losing weight. She felt increasingly weightless—feathery and sublime! Every inch of her skin tickled in the most pleasurable way and her mind poured out all its worries and doubts and fears. Her mind felt clear and warm and bright, as though it were basking before a glorious hearth. Nothing troubled her. Nothing confused her. In this moment she felt she could answer any question, only she had none to ask. Everything was as it was and required no explanation.

"This," said Suzy, knowing full well she was right, "is soul."

"Bingo!" cried Remmy.

She couldn't see him, amidst the great blinding light. But his voice registered from beside her, and she was glad that he was beside her and wanted him beside her always. "Now," he said, "pay attention."

Just then, a rush of images and sounds and thoughts railroaded straight at her, or at her mind (she could not tell the difference anymore). The images swooped at her and she saw it all. Everything. She saw a tunnel of pure light. She saw souls by the millions, by the tens and hundreds of millions, all of them disembodied orbs whirling through the tunnel like uncountable snowflakes.

"This is the Liminal Place," she heard Remmy say. "Or, as the Lucids would have it, the LP. It is a place midway between Dream and Reality. It is the gateway through which humans pass when they fall asleep. It is where the Dream Guard resides, watching over humans on their night journeys. It is accessible to every dreamer. If it wasn't, no one would ever awaken. It doesn't look like this anymore."

As Suzy continued to watch, all those millions and millions of bright shining orbs faded like stars at dawn. They went dark one by one. The luminous tunnel was still there, still swirling and gleaming every bit as attractively as before, but not a soul was partaking of it. What was breathtaking before was now eerie and desolate.

"Ever since the Great Deception," Remmy went on, "the LP has been lost. In Harold Dore's dream, the dream you are living in, the gateway has been hidden. That is why, no matter how lucid you become, you shall never wake up. If only it could be found…"

By degrees, the scene changed and Suzy found herself outside, on the very summit of Mount Nightlight. Remmy, his orange robe fluttering in the blustery wind, stood beside her. It was dawn and the sun shone above the valley.

Suzy looked in amazement at her own two hands. The dreambending journey she had taken, from flesh to soul and back to flesh, stole her breath and more: it made her appreciate how inexpressibly wonderful and mysterious life was, in direct contrast to the sleepwalkers and their narrow existence.

"That was some sand!" Suzy exclaimed.

"The best," said Remmy. "*Soul sand.*"

Then, slowly, he raised his golden eyes to the heavens. Suzy thought of the Liminal Place and how Remmy had called it his home.

"Do you miss it?" Suzy asked him. "The LP?"

"I miss my brethren," replied Remmy. "Before Phantos closed the gateway, some of the Dream Guardians, like myself, slipped through. We sought to help humanity, to fight the mares and find the LP. Ah, but it proved more daunting than any of us ever expected. Phantos and his minions hunted down the Dream Guard and imprisoned them in the Undreamt—an underworld of fear and illusion. I am the last one left."

"I'm so sorry, Remmy," and she reached out and hugged him about the middle.

Remmy stroked her flaxen hair, a single strand of which he would readily lay down his life to protect. All these bright and innocent youths, they were his greatest pleasure and, yes, his greatest weakness. He taught the Lucids to never let fear rule them, and yet he, a Dream Guardian, had this one fear: What would happen to the Lucids? What would happen to them if he was not around? Who would guide them and keep them safe? Of course, he knew about deep sleep and that death was an illusion, but that was not the point. They were the lightbearers: humanity's last hope. If their collective light went out, what then? Although he never showed it to the kids, he feared greatly for them. That on some infamous day Phantos would capitalize on this fear and use it to defeat him, Remmy accepted as his fate. That's how Phantos got you, through fear, and it would happen that way. Undoubtedly. The only question was when?

While Remmy was entertaining this troubling thought, Suzy was entertaining her own. She jerked away all of a sudden and said, "That's not my one question for the day, right? Oh, please, say it doesn't count! I've got something to ask you, something urgent!"

Remulus smiled at the pleading girl—he knew she was ready now; she was ready to ask him the big, important questions.

"Today," he said, "on the day of your lighting, you may ask me as many questions as your tongue can shake out."

"Are my parents alive? In Wakesville, are they alive?"

"Yes."

"What happened to them? Were they deep-sleeped?"

"They left in search of the Liminal Place. That is all I know."

"The LP?!" Suzy was astounded. How did her mom and dad know about the Liminal Place? "Were they Lucids too?"

"Not Lucids with a capital L. Tell me, what did they tell you they did for a living?"

"They taught at the university and, um, did research. Into sleep and memory, I think."

"They experimented with lucid dreaming, Suzy. They both were quite lucid, and I suspect their lucidity rubbed off on you. Anyway, they kept their research fairly private. It was not exactly academic and probably would have been laughed at by their colleagues. But they kept at it, exploring realms of dream that would have been better left unexplored. They needed help, though. They needed someone even more lucid than they, who could probe further into the realms of dream and report their findings. They interviewed many individuals, testing each one's lucidity, but were unsatisfied. Until, that is, a slender young man of twenty-one showed up at their lab.

"Harold Dore was gangly and unsociable, cut off from reality in direct proportion to the degree that he was immersed in dream. He was not only extremely lucid, though; he was ambitious too. He hailed from a prominent family, yet he never fit in among them and was considered the 'black sheep.' His feeling of unworthiness fostered in him a desire to prove himself, to attain power and prestige on his own terms. He had ambition. He had talent. He had everything your parents wanted in a candidate, except perhaps humility.

"How exactly Harold discovered the Undreamt is unknown. Perhaps a mare inveigled him into going there. Maybe he stumbled upon the gateway and fell through it, rather as a man tumbles down a staircase. Whatever the case, he met the arch demon Phantos. At this time, Phantos was trapped in the Undreamt. He had no way out. No means of inflicting his evil on mankind."

Suzy interjected. "But why does Phantos hate us so much?"

"He loathes humans because Morpheus, his twin and Chief Spirit of the Dream Guard, loves them. Morpheus holds as self-evident that humans have willpower and self-determination, and therefore, their dreams are theirs and theirs alone and should not be meddled with. Dream Guardians only intervene in people's dreams to ward off mares. That's it. We do not influence; we neither command nor demand. Phantos believes the opposite: that humans are meant to be enslaved. Morpheus follows the light; Phantos chases the dark. They serve different masters, in realms far beyond this one. But that is a story for another day."

"What happened next?" asked Suzy, who was taking full advantage of Remmy's generous offer to answer any and all of her questions.

"Phantos and Harold hatched a deal that would change the course of history. Phantos promised Harold eternal power. All he needed in exchange was Harold's mind—his dream. That, you see, was his ticket out of the Undreamt. Freed and as powerful as ever, Phantos put humanity to sleep. A vast and terrible slumber covered the planet like a shadow, and all succumbed to sleep. And when they reopened their eyes, behold, there was a world that looked real, sounded real, smelled and tasted and felt real! No one suspected a thing. According to their dreamfogged memories, they had always lived in the Unum and President Finkel had always been their leader. They had been suckered, duped, and none but we Dream Guardians and a few perceptive kids, with eyes to see, knew it."

Suzy took all this in. Silently, she processed everything Remmy had told her. She turned aside her head and peered down the mountain. She wasn't scared of heights anymore. She had overcome that. Would she be scared of Phantos, though? She didn't know, but she determined right there, at that very moment, on the top of Mount Nightlight, on the morning of her Lighting Ceremony, to do the impossible, the dangerous, to follow in her parents' footsteps and find the Liminal Place.

CHAPTER NINE

THE QUEST

Remulus fully approved of Suzy's decision to find the Liminal Place. It was what he had hoped she would do. He never would have asked her to go in quest of it, though. He never would have pushed her to do anything she wasn't prepared to do. This, you see, was the way of the Dream Guard—they respected the will of mankind and wished them to follow their own destiny.

Suzy figured, and Remmy concurred, that if the Liminal Place had been hidden, it was most certainly the doing of Harold. To track it down, she would have to go to him—to Finkel Mansion. Which she figured, and Remmy concurred, would entail untold dangers.

Suzy was surprised, however, when Remmy announced that he could not accompany her.

"But I need you!" she cried. "How could you let me go on my own?"

They were still on the mountaintop, and it was still morning.

"Not on your own. Your fellow Lucids will join you. Ask your most trusted friends and you will find able companions. As for the bulk of the Lucids, I must remain here and protect them. If I didn't..." he trailed off and his chest heaved a sigh. "Do you remember the story I told you of my first pupil?"

Suzy nodded. "Matthew, AKA Quicksand."

"Right. You had wanted to ask me something about him—I could tell. But your one question had been used up, and afterwards, you forgot. You may ask me now."

"What happened to him?"

"I left him. Only for a short while. We were living in an old subway tunnel then, and I ventured aboveground to look for youths who, like Matthew, could see beyond the counterfeit world. I left him. And the mares found him."

Suzy swallowed hard. She pressed him no more after that but did as he suggested and shared her plan with her closest friends: Sky, Orion, and Hermit. The trio who had rescued her from New Shiny City, who had showed her how to fly and use the dream items, and who were her teachers just as much as Remmy was. She had grown fond of them, each in their own special way: Orion's practical jokes and carefree attitude; Hermit's kindness and shy affection; even her bunkmate Sky, though she could be a taskmaster and was not as chatty as the others, had grown on her. Suzy was always glad to have Sky around. Sky was tough and focused, and, while the others were joking or lollygagging, she was often contemplating her next move like a chess player. Sky got things done. And, so, it was Sky whom Suzy asked first. If she agreed to go, the others would follow.

"Let me get this straight," said Sky, sitting up in bed and squinting at Suzy who lay overhanging the top bunk, her head angled down at Sky. "You want to fly to Finkel Mansion, where mares are as thick as the hairs of an alpaca, and go treasure-hunting for something we don't even know is there, or even exists? Only a twilighted newbie would suggest something as crazy as that."

"I'm a Lucid now," Suzy corrected.

"Whatever," said Sky, with an indifferent toss of her blue braids. "Don't you think we all had that same idea? And guess what? We all decided it was way too dangerous. It's the belly of the beast. It's the headquarters of Phantos, and you definitely don't want to run into him."

"Well, Remmy thinks it's a great plan," argued Suzy. "He supports it."

"Guess what else he supported? Every Lucid's decision, up until you, to NOT go off looking for the LP. If you haven't figured it out by now, Remmy doesn't tell people what to do."

Sky lay back down and, to signal that she was through speaking, turned her back on Suzy. This irked Suzy and she spat out, "Don't you want to go home? Back to Wakesville and your family? I mean, do you really want to be stuck in a dream your whole life?"

Suzy expected a quick rebuttal, something along the lines of "Of course not" or "Don't be stupid." Thus her surprise when Sky said, "And what if I do?"

It struck Suzy, just then, that she knew nothing about Sky, where she came from and who she was back in the real world. If hers had not been a particularly happy life, Suzy could well imagine how this magical mountain with its rollercoasters and flying pillows and bountiful banquets and singing fairies could be preferable. She knew she shouldn't pry, but she couldn't help asking, "Don't you miss your parents?"

"None of your business," snapped Sky. "Just shut up!"

Suzy retreated under the covers. Before long she heard Sky quietly snivel. Up until this moment, she didn't think Sky was capable of tears, so like granite was she.

The next day, while paddle-boating with Remmy in his grotto, Suzy learned the reason for Sky's unwillingness to return to Wakesville. Sky, or Trisha Weaver as she was called, had never known her parents. She spent her childhood pinballing among foster families, some good, some bad, some plain rotten. The experience hardened her. In Mount Nightlight, however, she had found a home that exceeded all the rest. Here, Sky was not alone. The Lucids might have parents who were deep-sleeped like Hermit's, or parents like Orion's who were still alive but so woefully asleep that it made living with them intolerable. ("They were gonna send me to Safety Enforcement Academy," Orion once complained. "Me, a Red Suit? It's like they wanted me to run away!") Whatever the situation, they were all orphans and Sky felt at home.

In view of Sky's personal history, Suzy understood the girl's reluctance. Yet the quest was too important to be abandoned simply because their doughtiest member declined. So, the very next morning, while breakfasting in the hall, Suzy confronted Orion and Hermit. Sky was present, of course, but she pretended not to be listening and concentrated instead on her banana-blueberry smoothie. Her blue hair hung before her face, forming a kind of curtain so that none could read her expression.

Orion, without hesitation, agreed to go. He slapped the table and said it was a "prime idea" and that he would love to give "them ghoul-faced nasties" a taste of his sand. He was not especially careful, thought Suzy—he didn't even mention Phantos or care to add him to the equation—but he was rash and easily excited, and this was enough.

Hermit was lukewarm on the idea, as lukewarm as the raisin oatmeal that he was eating, or was eating until he began to cogitate on all the dangers that Orion had overlooked. In the end, he said he would go if they all went together. "That's what friends do," he said, in his kind simple way. "They stick together."

At this, Suzy and Orion and Hermit all turned to Sky.

"Y'all hankering to be deep-sleeped," she spat out, hoping to frighten them.

Then, through a slit between her braids, she caught sight of Remmy. He was standing upon his high perch and looking, it seemed, directly down at her with his fire-bright eyes. He made no gesture and said nothing. He just gazed at her earnestly, then turned and strolled off among a flock of Nyxies.

Was it peer pressure or something Remmy conveyed with the majesty of his brilliant eyes, something not admonishing but uplifting and empowering, as though his golden gaze had announced, "You, Sky, are a hero!"? We shall never know. But the next thing out of Sky's mouth was, "So, when we leaving?"

They agreed to leave a week from Suzy's Lighting Ceremony. During the intervening days, preparations were made and plans were drawn up. The other Lucids, when word spread of their daring quest, felt a mix of emotions. Some thought they were batty; others thought they were heroic. Some felt envious and wished they could join them; others were only too glad to be sitting on the sidelines. Suzy noticed, and Orion, Hermit, and Sky did as well, that the other kids acted sweeter to them than they ever had before. They gave them frequent hugs, offered to do chores for them, shared food with them when there was plainly no need for it, and spoke of all the fun times they had had with them. To Suzy, it was unnerving.

In the days leading up to their departure, the four questers spent much time alone with Remulus. He gave them heaps of helpful advice—how to navigate through the Board, which was the capital district; how to evade the mares and Red Suits; and what to do should Phantos corner them (there was nothing to do, according to Remmy, except to cling to the Big Truth, that this world was a dream and there was nothing to fear, not even death). For all his hints and suggestions, Remmy could not answer the most important question: how would they find the Liminal Place? That was the fulcrum on which the success or failure of their journey depended, and it was a complete mystery.

On the morning of their farewell, the Lucids, one and all, piled into *The R.E.M. Express* and whooshed down and around the mountain tunnels. The shining Nyxies with their mothlike wings and big round eyes sang as they flew:

> *Off they go, quick to the race,*
> *To find the Liminal Place,*
> *Give a cheer, muster a shout,*
> *They'll put the mares to rout!*

Hear us well, our sweet farewell,
Till the breaking of the spell,
Stay wise, courageous, and true,
And always let the light guide you!

Finally, the rollercoaster slowed and halted, and the Lucids trooped the rest of the way on foot. There was a glimmer of sunshine ahead of them in the cave—the same cave through which Suzy had first entered Mount Nightlight. As they neared the daylight, the Nyxies began to fade. Their voices trailed off and they blinkered away. Ulala alone remained with the children and led them out of the cave and into the open air.

Remmy was already outside. He was sitting on the limestone shelf, in a lotus position, his whiskery nose pointed at the dawn as he picked his guitar. He was playing "Row, Row, Row Your Boat" again, using his claw as a plectrum and humming serenely. The Lucids amassed quietly at the mouth of the cave, listening to his warm, soulful voice. When he was finished, Suzy and her friends advanced toward him to say their goodbyes.

"I suppose it's time," said Remmy, setting down his guitar and rising to meet them.

"I suppose so," said Suzy. She was decked in the full panoply of a Lucid, with her jammies and gold sash and her pillow folded under her arm. In one of her bathrobe pockets was a wake mask, and in another pocket was a can of Dreamffiti. Sky, Orion, and Hermit were likewise outfitted.

"I hope," said Remmy, "you won't mind a little extra company?"

Suzy's heart soared with joy and relief. For she presumed that Remmy meant himself and that he had changed his mind and would join them on their quest. Instead, he stretched out his arm and there on his paw alighted Ulala. Suzy tried not to look disappointed, as it would surely offend the proud Nyxie.

"Remember," continued Remmy, "Nyxies are messengers. When mares are afoot in the dreams of mankind, the Nyxies are the ones who alert the Dream Guard. If you should become imperiled, I want to be told, and Ulala is best suited for that purpose."

Ulala bowed to Remmy, then shifted her bulbous eyes onto the four youths and said, primly, with the self-important air of an unappreciated martyr: "Worry not, children. I will only sing a little and when 'tis dark you shall be glad of my brilliance."

"You know we love you, ya cheeky sprite," said Orion, winking. Appeased, she settled upon his shoulder and petted his cheek with her glittery hand to show that he was her new favorite. Nyxies were always choosing new favorites and showering them with affection, mainly to chasten those who did not fully appreciate them.

"Now, then," said Remmy. "Is there anything you wish to ask me, before you go?"

The youths all looked at each other pensively, but none spoke. There was nothing left to ask, nothing left to review. Like a team of athletes who have trained at length, they wanted only for the whistle to blow and the game to begin.

"Very well," said Remmy. "One last thing: I know some of you are sad and perhaps hurt that I'm not accompanying you. But each of you has a can of Dreamffiti, and therefore, should you require my help, you need only shake and make and I'll be there—in pigmented liquid, anyway."

He bent and hugged Hermit, then Orion, then Sky, and finally Suzy. The heroes-to-be fluffed their pillows and climbed on. The wings beat excitedly, lifting Suzy and her friends up and away. As they rose into the air, the Lucids waved farewell and jumped up and down, while from every mouth came the cry of, *"Wake! Wake! Wake! Wake!"*

Remulus, stirred by the children's rallying cry, took up their chant. "WAKE!" he roared, throwing out his arms. "WAKE!" His thunderous cry seemed to shake the mountain loose of the earth, and the children stood in awe.

Suzy and her friends were long out of sight when the last Dream Guardian turned slowly away, his bright, burning eyes smoky with tears, and heaved a sigh in remembrance of his one great fear.

What will happen to them? he wondered.

What will happen to the Lucids?

CHAPTER TEN

TRAIN #213

Suzy and her companions flew to New Shiny City, to a neighborhood near Suzy's own. It was a small unremarkable neighborhood, only modestly cleaner and better-off than The Downsized, called Middletown. From Middletown, they planned to change out of their pajamas and board a train to Finkel Mansion. Of course, Suzy and her friends could have flown directly to the mansion and in a fraction of the time. Yet, as Remmy advised, their mission must be one of stealth. For if radar technicians happened to detect bizarre UFOs approaching the most important edifice in all the Unum, there would be sirens and screaming missiles galore.

They landed in an abandoned playground. Its wooden ladders and bridges and climbing walls were rotten and consumed by lichen. A barbwire fence surrounded the playground, and signs posted to the fence stated:

"CLOSED BY SAFETY ENFORCEMENT, DUE TO SPLINTERS."

Quickly they began to change. How weird it felt to Suzy, wearing her old school uniform again. The cheap, scratchy stockings chafed her skin, and her arms could barely bend in the rigid sleeves of her blazer. This done, she unpinned a few bags of dreamsand from her sash and deposited these in her jacket pocket. Then she stuffed the sash and her pajamas into her pillowcase and miniaturized the whole thing with a dollop of shrinkle-sprinkle. She laid the tiny pillow in her pocket, besides the velvet bags. The others did the same. They donned drab uniforms, hid their pajamas within their pillow-cases, and shrank the pillows to fit in their pockets. Sky's blue braids, which surely would have attracted unwanted attention among the populace, were concealed under a black beret. And, thus, the extraordinary foursome became an ordinary foursome.

"Gosh," said Hermit, gaping at his old school uniform, "this brings back memories!"

"Yeah," groaned Orion. "Bad ones."

A voice barked at them. "Hey, kids! Move along! This here's condemned, or maybe you don't read the signs!"

It was a Safety Enforcer, a Red Suit. His face unseen behind his tinted helmet shield, he banged his baton against the fence to frighten them. Sky wanted badly to stick her tongue out at him, and Orion would have loved nothing more than to braingrain him. Even Ulula, tucked in Orion's pocket, had the irrepressible urge to yank the dummy's ears.

However, as the children knew, they were not PG members anymore. They were proper schoolchildren and had to behave as such. So, they hung their heads and muttered apologies. The Red Suit, satisfied by their contrition, unlocked the gate and shooed them out, moralizing all the while on the dangers of splinters and how one child—somewhere, at some point, he couldn't recall exactly—had even died from a splinter wound.

The train station was a hop and a skip from the playground, and a good thing too. For, even over this short distance, Suzy and her friends garnered many stares from passersby. In the Unum, you see, it was neither customary nor lawful for children to be without adult supervision. Unattended children violated The Universal Right to Safety, Article 9: The Safety of Children. According to the law, unsupervised children might bruise their knees, or lick dirty candy wrappers, or get struck by lightning, or rained on, or bullied, or cheated, or seduced into the nefarious ranks of the Pajama Gang. Indeed, all manners of misfortune could result from children being children. Nevertheless, our four heroes arrived at Grand Unum Depot safe and sound, without having tasted trash or suffered electrocution.

The tickets were 1,500 digital Un-Coins per passenger, a steep fare even for the respectable types in Middletown. Suzy and her friends had the money, though, and more to spare. Money, as Remmy had taught them, was phony baloney in the dreamworld. It was as fake as Fakesville, and it was well-known that Finkel continually enlarged the supply of money, making it worth less and less. While the busy bees of the Unum toiled for their meager wages, Finkel dreamcasted *trillions* of Un-coins into existence and either spent them on hairbrained projects or lent them to his colleagues and friends. This being so, Remmy had seen no harm in adding a mere 1,000,000 Un-Coins to the money supply and placed these coins on credit cards for Suzy and her friends to use.

Before long, Train #213 was bulleting toward the capital. As Suzy stared out her window, the rot and ruin of New Shiny City stared back. The slums. The filthy factories. The greasy neon lights. The poor wallowing in the alleyways or huddling around their burning barrels. She wanted to fling open her window and shout to them, "Rejoice! Your nightmare's almost over!"

It was the fifth of May, yet it wasn't the sort of May that Suzy remembered. *What kind of May do I remember?* she asked herself. Of a sudden she turned to Hermit who was sitting beside her and sputtered, "Don't you remember May, what May used to be like, I mean? Buds and blossoms, singing birds and warm showers and fresh, earthy smells? Wasn't that how it was?"

She wasn't at all certain; she had no proof, but her gut told her it must be true. Often she had dreamed of this other world, which she now knew to be Reality, and her dreams had revealed tantalizing glimpses of a season surging with sun and vegetation, a season to be inhaled and savored and cherished.

Hermit shrugged indifferently. "It's the dream fog," he said. "Can't remember much before the GD."

By GD, he meant the Great Deception. And by dream fog, he meant the curious amnesia that affected everyone under the dream spell. Dream fog prevented people from remembering the real world and left them, at most, with fragments of memory—like scraps from a shredded book.

"But," Hermit added, "I do kinda sorta remember it being bluer."

"Yes!" insisted Suzy, latching onto this one vague memory from her friend. "The sky was bluer and the sea was bluer—as blue as Sky's braids, as blue as Remmy's fur!"

Hermit smiled at her and replied, matter-of-factly, as if he were stating 2 + 2 = 4, "Blue is the color of freedom."

Suzy, struck by Hermit's simple equation, as if he had uttered a profound mathematical theorem, echoed the young boy's words. "Blue is freedom." Then, in a whisper, Suzy vowed to herself, "We *will* have spring again."

Orion, who shared a seat with Sky, one row in front of Suzy and Hermit, poked his head over the back of his seat and grinned at Suzy. "A toast to spring!" he cried, raising his can of Slurpy Grape Soda, which he had purchased from the café car. "To the Great Awakening and the end of mare-dom!"

Sky shushed him, while Ulala, who lay in his jacket pocket, socked him in the chest. Orion hadn't a subtle bone in his body, and the sugar wasn't helping. His rowdy toast disturbed some of the passengers, including an elderly lady seated across from Suzy and Hermit. The lady was refined in style. Her emerald-green jacket and bowler hat, to say nothing of her parasol and pearl necklace, placed her in a stratum far above the average Unum citizen.

When this queenly lady heard Orion, she set her bifocals on the bridge of her nose and surveyed him and his companions sharply. Her look was withering. Her lips were pursed. Her eyes were squinched. But she said nothing. She only leaned on her parasol and, arising with some difficulty, hobbled off down the aisle.

The children thought nothing more of the incident. Maybe the lady disliked children. Maybe she was having a bad day. Who knew? And who cared? Two more stops and they would arrive in the capital. An ill-tempered granny was the very least of their worries.

Ah, but they were mistaken. For the lady had not only overheard Orion's careless speech but she had also recognized Suzy from the news. Unbeknownst to Suzy, ever since the fiasco at Unum Bites she had become the hated face of the Pajama Gang. Whenever the PG was mentioned in the news, Suzy's photo invariably accompanied the story, much to the chagrin of Aunt Millie and Uncle Norman.

Thus, when the old grouch got up and stumped away, she didn't merely change seats. She reported Suzy straightaway to the conductor, who phoned Safety Enforcement, which phoned Commissioner Jeffrey Sikman, who quit throwing darts at a poster of Suzy's face in his office and ran to his squad car and clocked 120mph to reach the next stop on the train before Suzy did.

Commissioner Sikman, joined by two high-ranking Red Suits, boarded the train. The conductor met them and pointed his finger, saying, "She's a few cars down, Commissioner." Sikman nodded and replied, "Get this train moving. When I throw the little buggers off, I want no survivors."

The conductor, who was human, gulped. There was a moment when it seemed he might question the morality of the order given to him. But Sikman, perceiving the man's hesitation, added in a confidential tone, "It is for our safety, good man."

Good man. Good woman. Good kid. These were Unum terms for patriots who did whatever Finkel's government demanded of them. It was a mind trick, of course. Who didn't want to be good? Who didn't want to be safe? The conductor wanted to be both good and safe, and he hurried to the controls to accelerate the train such that no child would survive being thrown from it.

Sikman prowled the aisle like a hunter. His dark, colorless eyes swerved from face to face, and his pointy ears wriggled on either side of his black cap, listening for children.

Now, by pure dumb luck, as Sikman and the officers were about to cross from one car to the next, Orion happened to exit a nearby bathroom. He had pounded a liter of Slurpy Grape and all this carbonated soda had to go somewhere. As he slid the bathroom door open and stepped out, he glanced over his shoulder and through the plexiglass partition between cars beheld the tall, ugly police commissioner.

"Nasties!" gasped Orion. Then, spinning on his heels, he hurried back to where his friends were sitting and repeated this intelligence. "Nasties!"

This, and a twitch of his head in the direction of the approaching lawmen, proved sufficient warning. Suzy, Hermit, and Sky sprang to their feet. Confusion ensued, with Hermit saying, "Let's up-and-away!" and Sky arguing, "There's no time!" and Orion squawking, "Nasties! Bat-faced nasties!"—until Suzy, seeing little point in all this back-and-forth, took off running.

Did she have a plan? Not in the slightest. But the others believed she did and followed her, until they all stumbled breathlessly into the café car. At which point Suzy confessed what we already know, that she didn't have a plan and ran simply because that was the only thing to do.

Well, now they couldn't run anymore—the café car was the last car on the train. Suzy looked helplessly to Sky who, understanding, took command. She told them to *grandsand* their pillows, and then she threw herself at the emergency window.

The pimply café attendant behind the counter saw what Sky was up to and yelled at her: "Um, excuse me, you can't do that! It's, um, against The Universal Right to Safety, Article, um, 114, Section D, Subsection Three, Concerning, um, the Emergency Windows of Trains, Buses, and, um, Other Public Transit…"

Ulala had had enough of the café attendant—his sound was mindless drivel, the very opposite of the Nyxies' beauteous songs, and she couldn't stand to hear it. She sprang from the breast pocket of Orion's blazer, where she had been hiding, and fluttered over to the server and closed his lips with a forceful jerk of her luminous limbs. The server went cross-eyed trying to see the little being who had silenced him; then, seeing her, his eyes went all wibbly-wobbly and he fell in a faint.

Now, with the attendant out of the picture, there was only one other person in the café car; and this one person, sitting alone at a table and attracting no notice whatsoever from our four friends, was the old lady in the emerald-green jacket and hat. We shall return to her in a moment, but for now observe her, sitting there broodingly, her beady eyes hovering above the rim of her coffee cup and glaring at our heroes…

By now, the Lucids had accomplished two important tasks: Sky had managed to unlatch and open the emergency window, while Suzy, Orion, and Hermit had managed to enlarge their pillows to normal size.

"OK!" cried Sky, waving Orion over, "you first!"

Clutching the flapping pillow to his chest, Orion whooped "Excito!" and dove like a skydiver from the speeding train.

"Hermit!" shouted Sky. "You're next!"

Hermit, with less gusto and less grace than Orion, executed the same means of escape: he hugged his pillow to his tummy, then flopped out the window, screaming.

"Come on!" Sky urged Suzy, motioning her forward. "It's pillow time!"

But Suzy tossed her flight pillow to Sky, saying, "You first!"

Oh, how this irritated Sky! Being the oldest of the bunch and therefore the group's unofficial protector, Sky felt entitled to be the last to leave. She had the urge to grab Suzy by her hair and throw her out the window—with her pillow, of course. And, yet, there was something magnanimous in Suzy's gesture which resonated with Sky, something she respected and could not refuse. So, only scowling a little, she pointed to her own pillow lying on the floor and said, "Don't just stand there, Snoozy—grab mine and go!"

With a shout of "Excito!", Sky left the train and Suzy was alone. Or at least she thought she was. As she went to retrieve Sky's pillow, the tip of a parasol pinned the pillow to the floor. The genteel lady in the green jacket, grasping her parasol handle with both hands, let out a hoarse cackle, which was far too deep for a woman or even a man.

"My, my," snorted the lady, "aren't we in haste, dear child?"

"Let go!" Suzy demanded as she tugged at the pillow. "What are you doing? Let go!"

But it was little use, for the old lady was incredibly strong. She leaned her weight against her parasol and by this means guaranteed that the pillow, and Suzy, would never leave the train.

Now, Ulala, as you might recall, was still in the car and saw all this transpire and did not approve of it one bit. Summoning her brightest light, she shot like a comet toward the lady.

Harassed by the Nyxie (Ulala had knocked off her hat and was now pulling vigorously at her gray hair), the lady stumbled backwards. Suzy, meantime, reached into Sky's pillowcase, fetched her wake mask, and slipped it on. Then, glancing at the lady, she discovered why the lady was so strong and so mean too. For she was not a lady at all; she was a hideous, ox-faced, bat-winged, slimy, slug-bodied beast!

In other words, a mare.

"*Snooooozy!*" trilled Ulala, singing even as she did battle with the creature. "*Fly away now! Go and I'll fight the cow!*"

While Ulala dove repeatedly at the mare like an angry hornet, Suzy ripped off her mask and picked up her pillow and…

Suddenly, she was lifted into the air.

Lifted by her neck.

A black gloved hand, the hand of Commissioner Sikman, clutched her by the scruff of her neck.

In his other hand, he had caught poor Ulala. He squeezed her mercilessly. With a sideways glance, Suzy saw Ulala's colors fade and fade, until it seemed the Nyxie would be snuffed like a candle.

"I am not certain which I despise more," Sikman remarked to the granny mare. "A tattle-telling fairy, or an impudent child who thinks she can defy Lord Phantos."

"I'm prejudiced against the Nyxie," growled the old lady, as she touched her hanky to the tiny scratch marks on her forehead.

Sikman carried Suzy and Ulala, one like a rodent and the other like a bug, toward the open window. Suzy writhed and flailed, trying to slip free. Outside the window the city whipped past her, a terrifying blur of concrete and graffiti. Suzy felt the cold rush of wind and the cold sting of death. She was panicky and very afraid.

"The Big Truth, the Big Truth," she uttered the phrase over and over, like a prayer. She shut her eyes, and everything went dark, and in another moment, everything went silent.

"The Big Truth, the Big Truth," Suzy repeated.

She needed to remember what Remmy had taught her. She needed to believe, to believe with all her heart, that Sikman, as terrible as he was, could never hurt her. She needed to trust that this crazy world was just a crazy dream, and that she could dream too.

There was a tumult. A crash!

Sikman lost his footing and launched backwards against a booth of the café car. Screams and shouts erupted throughout the train. The scenery outside the windows, had you looked just then, would have revealed no buildings and no chimneys, only cumulus and wispy stratus clouds. The train, you see, had peeled off the rails and was now chuffing forth at a perfect ninety-degree angle from the earth. The sharp, reeling trajectory of a rocket! Drawn aloft by some intangible force which only Suzy and Ulala and the mares understood, the train rose through the air.

The instant that Sikman smacked against the booth, he groaned and released his captives. Ulala, regaining her luminosity, cracked Sikman across the cheek with her open palm. Suzy, less interested in retribution than the proud Nyxie, searched for Sky's pillow and snatched it as it skidded past her in a cascade of coffee cups, suitcases, and cell phones.

Suzy fluffed the pillow, and both she and Ulala clung to it as it carried them up through the body of the train, from the café car to the next car to the next car. They climbed higher and higher, until they reached the engine room. There, the conductor sat blubbering over his controls, lamenting that he had done something wrong and that this was the reason Train #213 had become a space rocket. Suzy, kneeling on her magic pillow, flung open an exit door and zipped off into the mist. Ulala, with her own two wings, followed suit.

Upon Suzy's departure, the train rose no more. Suspended for a heartbeat at its apex, it sank back down and caused the luggage and food items and, indeed, Sikman and the granny mare to plunge in the other direction. The train resettled onto the track rather gently, however, with nothing more jarring than a runway bounce.

A collective sigh then passed from the lips of every passenger, followed by excitable chatter concerning the extraordinary flying train. It was impossible! Unbelievable! "Like a dream!" cried one astute man, who had recorded the entire episode on his phone. He then uploaded the video to the social network, Unum Book, where it was rapidly shared and viewed over 1,000,000 times.

In response, Unum Book swiftly banned the video.

In further response, Unum News reported that Train #213 did not *really* fly into the troposphere. Rather, the passengers and other witnesses had been duped, once again, by the wily Pajama Gang. It was a case of trickery, mass hallucination, and nothing more. Move along, folks. Nothing to see here. And everyone, including the astute man, accepted the lie as truth.

CHAPTER ELEVEN

A JOLLY GOOD FINKEL

Once Train #213 was out of sight, the children alighted beside the track and recapped the terrifying ordeal they had just endured. Orion and Hermit, far from being discouraged, were more confident than ever that they would find the Liminal Place, for they had Snoozy Suzy— who could, apparently, dreamcast trains to the moon and back.

Suzy blushed in modesty—she herself barely understood it— and credited their eldest member, saying, "Well, it was Sky's idea to escape through the emergency window." Then, feeling a sharp pinch on her arm, Suzy remembered to also honor the Nyxie. "And it was Ulala who valiantly and heroically fought the mare." Ulala quit pinching Suzy and flew to her shoulder, where she stroked the girl's cheek and sighed melodically. She really adored the adverbs Suzy had used.

Overall, the Lucids and their fairy were in good spirits and ready to resume their mission. In the distance they beheld a monument—The Pillars of Safety—and they knew from Remmy that these four obelisks surrounded Finkel Mansion.

They were still in their school uniforms which, as you recall, served as disguises. They needed only to shrink their pillows and pocket them to avoid suspicion. This done, they hoofed it through a patch of weedy foxtails, past a hobo camp, and down a gravelly hill into New Shiny City.

The capital district of New Shiny City was named "the Board" for two reasons, one obvious and one subtle. The obvious reason was that this area of the city was an enormous chessboard. Each square mile of the Board consisted of 64 squares, said squares being either black or white. This look required constant upkeep, and on almost any day, barring holidays, crews could be seen outside with their squeegees rolling on new coats of paint. The subtle reason derived from the fact that a board is a term denoting a group of people who govern a company or institution. And Finkel and his administration were certainly, in this sense, a board. They controlled the world.

It was the first time that Suzy and her friends had ever visited this part of the city, and they were agog at the fabulous 3D chessboard. More peculiar still was how eerily depopulated the Board was. Besides the Red Suits, people were few. And when they did appear, whether riding in the backs of self-driven taxis or emerging from the automatic doors of monolithic corporate offices, they invariably wore business suits and toted briefcases. These people looked different somehow from your average sleepwalker. It was, Suzy decided, their eyes. Theirs were not glazed over and half asleep, but instead appeared alert and intelligent. Suzy, struggling to account for this difference, pegged them for mares. Orion bet her a bag of sand that they were not. To settle the matter, Sky donned her wake mask and stole a peek at a man and a woman as they climbed into a taxi.

"Well," Sky reported, "you're both wrong. The man is a mare; the woman is human."

Sky went on to explain to Suzy that some humans collaborate with mares. These humans knowingly and willingly work against the interests of humanity, spreading fear, lies, and poverty. In exchange, the mares reward them with immense wealth and important titles. The Lucids called them *humares* and held them in even lower regard than the mares—which said a lot.

"Humares," Orion sneered, spitting on the ground. "Traitors! Sellouts! I'd braingrain the whole lot of 'em, I would!"

This sobering lesson being over, Suzy and her friends walked on. They crossed black squares and white squares, then more black squares and more white squares. Perhaps only a pawn that has been queened could appreciate the drudgery of their progress. About midday, they reached Finkel Mansion.

Outside the gated mansion, a massive parade was underway. A motorcade of limousines and armored tanks rolled through the square, to the shrieking delight of a crowd thousands and thousands deep. The people waved signs and blew horns and threw confetti and hugged their neighbors. There were news cameras everywhere. News drones thronged the sky like a hatching of gnats.

The children edged up to the crowd. As they did so, the clamor became overwhelming—the screams verged on the hysterical and horns blared as if the city were on fire. What really was happening was this: President Art Q. Finkel was gracing the people with his presence.

He was larger than life, a giant among elves, strong, cool, and confident. His hair was a lustrous black, and his gray business suit and red tie spoke to his businesslike demeanor. His shoulders were broad, his chest was broad, his chin was broad and cleft in the middle. His teeth were white, his skin tropically tan. Ruggedly handsome, he could have been a movie star, perhaps one of those action heroes that Uncle Norman idolized. He had no faults. No defects. No weaknesses. He was the face of the Unum, and the Unum was perfect.

Finkel rode upon a flatbed, a huge float, which was pulled by an armored jeep. Generals of the military, each decorated with more stars and trinkets than a Christmas tree, stood at his side. And behind him, nailed to the float, was the hideous, gaping, one-eyed head of the monster called Nemesis.

Yes, Nemesis, the terror of the Unum, fear itself, was dead. It had been slain. Decapitated. Eureka! And it was all thanks to the dapper gentleman in the gray suit! President Finkel laced his hands together and waved them over his gelled hair, drawing ecstatic cheers from the crowd.

"After years of collective suffering," cried Finkel, his voice bolstered by the microphone clipped to his lapel, "after years of sacrifice and austerity, after years of clutching our young ones whenever we beheld the frothy sea, we can sigh in collective relief. From this day forth, the ocean which separated the peoples of the Unum shall separate them no more. From this day forth, the Unum is ever closer, ever united in its oneness. For the dreadnaught beast," and here he gestured grandly to the big, ugly fish head, "is dead! Long live the Unum! Long live the Unum!"

Unable to contain their happiness, the crowd broke out into song:

> *For he's a jolly good Finkel,*
> *For he's a jolly good Finkel,*
> *For he's a jolly good Finkel,*
> *Which nobody can deny!*
> *Which nobody can deny!*

Their jubilation was contagious. Even Suzy, who ought to have known better, caught it. Thoughtlessly, she began to hum along...until Sky elbowed her.

"It's all theater!" Sky told Suzy. She was shouting an inch from Suzy's face to be heard over the crowd. "It's not even the right size! The head should be way bigger—like, twenty times bigger! Yet there it is, somehow, on a float. How convenient!"

Sky's observation was spot on. And what startled Suzy was not merely how thousands of sleepwalkers could overlook a detail so important. What startled her was that she herself had done so. It was easy to think critically while living at Mount Nightlight; here, in the heart of Fakesville, one had to keep her wits about her.

They got right to work. Theirs was a mission of stealth, as you might recall. They could not waltz up to the front gate and beseech the men in the dark suits and sunglasses to please let them in. No, that would never work. What they did instead was this: they jostled through the crowd and ducked behind one of the cars in the motorcade. No one was looking at this car. Every eye was glued to Finkel. Huddled behind this car, they shrinkle-sprinkled themselves. Miniaturized, they donned their cozy pajamas and gold sashes and buckled their pillows to their backs. All of this was accomplished in a minute.

The men in the dark suits and sunglasses who guarded the gate of Finkel Mansion were not accustomed to stopping and interrogating mites, spiders, or any other critter for that matter. They hardly ever glanced at their shiny black shoes, except to tie them. And so it was that the four children, each roughly an inch in height, and one tiny Nyxie scuttled right past the security detail. They ran up the walkway, crawled under the front door, and zipped past the metal detectors to encounter a door of bulletproof plexiglass. As the door slid open to admit several cabinet members, they scurried inside.

Finkel Mansion was a palace of unequaled luxury. The walls were papered with gold filigree. The chandeliers glittered with diamonds. The marble floor was laid with red carpet. The halls contained more sculptures, paintings, and tapestries than a museum. You must remember that President Finkel, i.e. Harold Dore, could pull money out of thin air. Luxury was literally never out of reach.

What you might not have guessed about Finkel Mansion was that its layout was purposefully designed to be confusing. Corridors branched off from one another, leading to more hallways and more doors. It reminded Suzy of a hedge maze, and when she squeaked out this thought (her voice had shrunk along with her bones), the others agreed.

"We're never gonna find Finkel's office!" griped Orion.

Suzy had an idea. "What if we ask someone?"

They looked at her as if she had gone quite mad. But when she explained that the person they would ask would first be braingrained, they warmed considerably to her idea.

Orion, who had a somewhat unhealthy obsession with braingrains, volunteered for the job. He jumped onto his pillow, soared over to one of those black-suited goons, and slugged him in the back. As the man spun around, thinking a fly was harassing him, Orion chucked a fistful of sand into his face. The security officer instantly slackened. He stared woodenly at the thumb-sized boy, like a puppet. Orion ordered him to "lead the way to the President's office", which he did, and to "be quick about it", which he was. Then the security officer, upon Orion's further direction, left to go empty his bank account and give all his money to the poor.

Finkel's office was as huge as it was creepy. Despite there being no windows, a graveyard chill pervaded the space. Forming a ring around the office were bronze statues, which resembled fanged and fearsome gargoyles, but which the Lucids knew were actually mares. The floor was tiled in black-and-white squares, much like the Board itself. On Finkel's desk were three computer monitors, stacks of documents, and a coffee mug. There were also bookcases; an oval dressing mirror; and, behind Finkel's desk, a mural depicting the symbol of the Unum: the blue dot contained in the red circle.

President Finkel was not here, nor were his staffers. There wasn't a single living thing in the President's office, save for one Nyxie and four courageous children.

They had made it!

In this very room they hoped to find the portal to the Liminal Place, or at least a clue that indicated where it was.

They decided to split up and search the office, but to remain shrunken lest a hidden security camera expose them. Hermit jogged off toward the bookshelves. Orion, attracted by their sheer ugliness, went to inspect the mare statues. Sky drew toward the mirror, while Suzy soared on her shrunken pillow to the top of Finkel's desk. Ulala, meanwhile, alighted near the door. Hers was an important job, that of the lookout.

They had only recently begun their sleuthing when Ulala harked voices in the hall. Her entire body flashed like lightning as she whistled to the children. Abandoning their searches, the Lucids hid wherever was convenient: Hermit squeezed himself in between two books; Orion crouched behind the pedestal of one of the statues; Sky dove underneath the feet of the mirror; and Suzy ducked behind the coffee mug.

As the voices grew louder, Ulala decided that she too must hide and betook herself to the chandelier. She was in such haste, however, with her head corked around and watching the door, that she accidentally flew into a cobweb. The sticky web sprawled among the diamond fixtures. Ulala squirmed in the web, but it was no use— she was caught. She thought of crying out to the Lucids for help, but, alas, she could not do this either. Because just then the door opened…

"Thank you again!" Finkel said to a group of worshipful pages. They were teenagers in gray blazers and red ties, exactly like the kind Finkel wore. They were little Finkels. "Thank you for your unflagging support," he told them, backing into his office. "We have prevailed against a great foe today. Thank you, thank you and goodbye!"

The pages were singing, "For he's a jolly good Finkel! For he's a jolly good Finkel!" as the object of their devotion shut the door on them and locked it.

His back against the door, Finkel was seen to smile. "A jolly good Finkel," he muttered to himself, laying emphasis on the word "good."

Then, in a baffling turnabout of emotion, Finkel frowned and sighed and stumped to his desk. His back was bent, his head downcast. He sank, rather than sat, in his chair and covered his face with his hands. Then the great Art Q. Finkel, leader of the Unum and the slayer of Nemesis, began to cry.

His muffled sobs were so altogether unexpected to Suzy that she momentarily forgot the danger of being caught and peeked out from behind the mug. Sure enough, Finkel was sulking. He was draining his nose into tissue after tissue.

If only the people of the Unum could see him now! thought Suzy. *Then they'd know he wasn't perfect but just as human as the rest of us!*

Suzy remained watching as Finkel swept the tissues into a waste basket and pulled open a drawer. From this drawer he removed a pair of scissors. These were no ordinary office scissors. For one, they were jumbo-sized—more on par with garden shears. And secondly, the handles were made of polished gold and embossed with rubies.

Equipped with these exquisite cutters, Finkel rose from his chair and skirted around his desk to the center of the room. There he lingered, for a full three minutes, staring at the scissors he held and faintly moaning. Whatever he was about to do, he seemed to dread it. Then, as the third minute drew to an end, he raised his scissors and began to cut.

Suzy, her eyebrows scrunching in amazement, gasped.

Hermit, watching from the bookshelves, went pale.

Orion, poking his head above the pedestal, mouthed phrases of incredulity, like "What the mare?" and "Well, wake me twice!"

Over by the mirror Sky shook her blue braids side to side, unwilling to believe what she was seeing.

For what Finkel cut was none other than the very fabric of the dreamworld.

The steel blades clipped and snipped through empty space. As the fabric of the dream sagged and fell away like a paper cutout, there appeared a black hole.

The hole, about four feet in diameter, billowed thick black smoke. It was as if there were a volcano on the other side of it. The smoke forced Finkel to stutter away, gagging, his nose buried in his shirt collar.

Then, from the black hole, a figure emerged.

It was a small figure in a solid black outfit, said outfit covering hands and feet and terminating in a pointy cap. The only part of the figure not covered by this black suit was the face, which was painted with white powder. Notwithstanding the black lips and black eyeshadow, which outlined the eyes in the shape of diamonds, the face was fresh and pretty. The young lady's monochromatic look was completed by her ruff, this being striped black and white. The wand she held resembled the kind that stage magicians sometimes employ—thin and black, with a white tip. She was a magician. She was a jester. She was a damsel with an ingenuous smile, from which no mischief or evil could be suspected.

Suzy certainly suspected nothing of the sort.

And, yet, as the young woman skipped lightly from the infernal hole, President Finkel shrank onto his knees.

He bowed his head and, turning pale with fright, though not as pale as the young woman's face, exclaimed, "Lord Phantos, master, it is ever good to see you!"

CHAPTER TWELVE

PHANTOS

An ingénue with a painted face and black one-piece suit…this was not anywhere close to the portrait of Phantos that Suzy had imagined. A horned, red-skinned devil or else a cloaked and hooded skeleton, surely Phantos had to be as terrifying as one of these? Surely, the big, bad demon of whom Remmy spoke could not be this pretty, little jester?

Phantos, if such she really was, approached Finkel.

"Master, why this form?" complained Finkel, looking her over. "It doesn't suit you at all."

"More the better!" tittered the jester, as she gamboled and pirouetted about him. "Nothing so pleases me as illusion. Under my reign, that which is perceived shall never be that which is." Here, she landed in front of him and added in a tone as dark as her lips: "I could do worse, you know."

"I know," he said, swallowing a mouthful of fear.

"Besides," she went on, more cheerfully, "in this dreamshow, no one is what he is. What matters substance? What matters shape? Those are human concerns! We of the Undreamt laugh at them, for we know the true nature of existence is a stage and all beings, shadow puppets."

"But even shadows," argued Finkel, with a hint of resentment, "require light. Otherwise, they'd cease to exist."

If there was anything that perturbed Phantos, if there was anything that pained and aggravated the arch demon at all, it was plainspoken truths—truths that could not be hid, destroyed, or countered. And what Finkel just spoke was so true, so perfectly true, that Phantos could only crinkle her mouth like a caged wolf and change the subject.

"Harold Dore," she said, wagging her finger at him, "you have gone and done a bad thing."

"I couldn't help myself," he whined. And peering up into the pretty face of the demon, he cried, "If I don't show the people that Art Finkel means business, that he can get things done now and then, they'll lose faith in me—they will!"

"You had our big beast killed," she went on, unmoved by his excuse. "And did you consult me, hmm? Did you even *think* to consult me, your maestro, your ringmaster, me who runs this dreamshow?!"

Finkel's chiseled face dropped. He stared at the checkered floor like a chastened schoolboy. "I'm sorry, I am, but…there was a moment there, when the crowd was singing together and looking happy, so indescribably happy, that I thought: *Why must it be so?*"

He launched off his knees and onto his feet, whereat all his fear and shame sloughed away from him like dead skin. He had been to the proverbial mountain and had a vision, and he announced it to Phantos with the zeal of a prophet: "Why must we frighten the people? Why must we tell them what to think? Why must we darken their skies? Why must we pollute their water? Why must we overwork them? Why must we over-police them? Why must we feed them lie after lie after lie! We control the dream, don't we? Well, then, we could make it whatever we want! We could make it wonderful! A living utopia! We'd still be at the top, that would not change, not one bit. We would still rule, only benevolently and mercifully, with liberty and prosperity for all!"

Suzy—and, doubtless, her cohorts hiding behind the mirror, the books, and the sculpture—was simply amazed to hear these words coming from President Finkel. Had he not put every last human to sleep? Had he not sucked everyone into his dream and enthroned himself as king? Had he not, as President, eroded the freedom and happiness of the people? And, yet, here he was advocating on their behalf, going to bat for them as if he really cared!

Phantos was not of the same persuasion. She interrupted Finkel with a ferocious growl that belied her dainty form. She thrust her magic wand at him, and, by this means, flung him off his feet.

Finkel was thrown toward the dressing mirror. Suzy thought for sure he would smack against it and shatter the glass into a hundred jagged pieces. Instead, he jerked to a halt several inches from its reflective surface, his suede shoes dangling above the floor.

"Look!" shrieked Phantos, from across the room. "Look and remember what you were!"

And in the mirror Art Finkel was Harold Dore—and Suzy knew it was so, because the man in the reflection matched the description Remmy had given her.

Now, I must be perfectly honest: Harold was not handsome. Even Suzy, who was more forgiving than the author, thought this so. Harold was nothing that Finkel was and everything that he wasn't. He was gangly and boney, with haunted eyes and a wisp of a chin. He was as flimsy as Finkel was firm; as moon-white as Finkel was sun-browned; as frowning and friendless as Finkel was smiling and beloved. His hair was buzzed short, his glasses were thick rectangles, and he wore black jeans and a black T-shirt with the words "I'D RATHER BE SLEEPING" printed across its front, followed by a string of Z's.

"Harold Doormat," taunted Phantos, smirking at the lank man in the mirror. "Hairbrained Harold. The perennial loser of the Dore family, until he met me. We cut a deal. We formed an alliance, whose ultimate goal only he and I and my minions will ever know. Remind me, Mr. Doormat, of our founding principles."

Finkel, in anguish before his true self, clenched his eyes as he recited the following:

"The Dream must deceive.

"The Dream must enslave.

"The Dream must never end.

"If the Dream no longer deceived, the dream would no longer enslave; if the Dream no longer enslaved, the Dream would end."

With a satisfied smirk, Phantos flicked her wand and hurled Finkel into his desk chair. Suzy dashed around the mug yet again, dreading that one of them might discover her. She was terribly frightened. Her poor heart quailed. At the same time, she was smart enough to understand that this tete-a-tete between Finkel and Phantos might prove revealing. Already she had witnessed scissors that could cut open portals to other realms. Might this same tool be used to reach the Liminal Place?

"Now, then," said Phantos, hopping onto the desk and crossing her legs, "let's see what's in store for the good people of the Unum."

She held up her right hand, which was clothed in the same black suit as the rest of her body, and frisked her fingers together. At once, a playing card popped up from her palm. She dropped the card onto the desk. "Since you've killed Nemesis," she went on, "a new enemy is needed, and these waifs will more than suffice."

Suzy, crawling under the handle of the mug, peeked at the card face. The card, which was the Four of Hearts, depicted a group of Lucids. Surely it was a coincidence that the card had four Lucids on it and Suzy and her friends made four Lucids. All the same, Suzy got goosebumps.

Finkel shot Phantos a look of surprise. "But no one takes the Pajama Gang seriously."

"Don't they? While you were parading around with a giant fish head—which, by the way, was too small to be plausible—these punks made a passenger train go off the rails."

"Into a ditch?"

"Into a cloud."

"Oh," was all that Finkel had to say.

Phantos leaned toward him and bopped him on the noggin with her wand. "Your kind, Harold, are beginning to talk. To think. To question."

"The Dream must deceive," Finkel recited, nodding in comprehension of the threat.

"We must make an example of these streetwise urchins," declared Phantos. "Otherwise, more may join their cause and seek after the truth."

"But how do we take them?" interjected Finkel. "Their hideout is unknown."

"Easy!" cried Phantos. "The next brat in pajamas we catch, we squeeze her…" and with her hands, she mined the crushing of a tiny Lucid, presumably one under the influence of shrinkle-sprinkle, such as Suzy and her friends were now. "We torture her until she must talk. She'll spill everything, including the whereabouts of her friends."

There arose in Finkel's mind one major hurdle, one Jupiter-sized obstacle to the success of this plan. He didn't have to vocalize it, because just then Phantos performed another sleight of hand and threw a second card onto the desk. This one, which was the Ace of Hearts, showed an image of Remulus.

"Don't you worry your pretty head about *him*," said Phantos.

"He will protect them," warned Finkel.

"Oh, I'm counting on it!" shrieked Phantos, rubbing her palms together. "His love for them will be his downfall; his love for them will be his end!" She elaborated no further on this point. Her demented hyena giggle was enough to convince Finkel that she would, at the appropriate hour, overcome the last Dream Guardian.

"Ever shrewd, master," said Finkel. "Ever shrewd."

But his praise sounded hollow. All the passion he radiated earlier, when he spoke of reforming the dream and uplifting the people, was gone. Suzy heard the difference and wondered at it and stored it in the back of her mind.

"Now," said Phantos, "let us inform the inner circle."

At these words, the statues of the mares that ringed the room were statues no more. The nine bronze gargoyles were now living things, panting and salivating and eyes red-glowing! Orion, who, as you recall, was hiding behind the pedestal of one of these mares, was nearly squished underfoot as the creature shuffled forward. They were huge hulking demons, horned and winged and evil. And, yet, in the next second, in a blink of an eye, they were humans. Many wore stylish business suits; two wore military uniforms; one wore a tiara and red gown; and the final one wore the tunic of some religious order.

"Today," Phantos began, addressing the inner circle, "marks the beginning of a new campaign…"

But Phantos never finished her thought, for just then the diamond chandelier above them swayed and tinkled as if by the wind.

Only there were no windows, and hence no draft, and hence it was a most puzzling occurrence, unless you happened to be Ulala. For if you were she, you would know that the chandelier was moving because you were moving. Ulala was wriggling to unstick herself from the cobweb.

Phantos observed the chandelier rocking to and fro. She scooted off the desk and crept toward the center of the room, her shadowy eyes never leaving the chandelier.

With a flutter of her wings, Ulala tore free of the webbing. She was so focused on removing herself from the web, she grew careless and forgot that a far more dangerous foe was afoot than a spider. No sooner had she extricated herself than Phantos, employing her wand, hurled Ulala onto the desk for Finkel to see.

"A Nyxie!" he shrieked.

He recoiled as if the tiny woman were a rat.

"We have been infiltrated!" shouted Phantos.

Ulala, pinned on her back, could not move a muscle, try though she might. Phantos's magic was stronger and stickier than any spiderweb. Ulala shined her brightest light, but it was hardly a deterrent to the powerful demon. Equally ineffective were the colorful curses that Ulala directed at Phantos, which we cannot repeat here.

"Afraid of spiders, are we, my wee little friend," jeered Phantos. "Well, then…"

Phantos stretched her fist toward Ulala and, unfurling her fingers, unleashed a tarantula. The big, hairy spider sprang at Ulala. Suzy couldn't bear to witness her companion eaten alive. She sprinkled grandsand over herself and began to enlarge. Within a few seconds, she was an average-sized girl standing unceremoniously on the desk of the President. No matter, she hiked her foot—the one that enjoyed the comfort of a shoe—and stomped the spider.

And, yet, when Suzy lifted her shoe, there was nothing there. No squashed spider, just Finkel's polished mahogany.

Sky, Orion, and Hermit took courage from Suzy's example and, regaining their normal statures, came out into the open. They dashed past the members of the inner circle and huddled beside Suzy.

"The Pajama Gang!" cried Finkel. "Here, in my mansion! The Pajama Gang!" He found this incredible. He couldn't fathom the madness that would prompt four kids to willingly enter the headquarters of Evil. Phantos was less surprised than gratified. "Now we shall learn their secrets!" she gasped, with a diabolical grin.

"Run!" cried Sky and the four of them—five if you counted Ulala—made a break for the door. Yet when Sky flung open the door, they were met with conflagration. A wall of blazing fire! Sky grounded her bath slippers, and the others piled up behind her.

"Going so soon?" cooed Phantos. "But we've so much to discuss."

"Your days are numbered!" Sky cried, swiveling around and crooking a finger at Phantos. "People are gonna wake up, and when they do, you'll be vaporized! Converted back into nothing, which is what you are! How's that for a discussion?"

"On second thought," said Phantos and she flicked her wand at Sky, freezing her in a block of ice. The mares chuckled grimly, and Finkel looked away.

Now Orion, seeing his good friend encased in ice, became absolutely livid. He tore a green bag from his sash and hurled it at the demon, raging, "Suck sand, clown-face!"

But the braingrains had no effect on Phantos except to dirty her outfit. Dusting off her shoulder, she pointed her wand at the boy and rendered him unto stone. Again, the mares chuckled. Again, Finkel looked away.

Angry tears stung Hermit's eyes, yet he was not so bold as to insult Phantos. From this, and the way he trembled, Phantos surmised that the boy in the baby-blue pajamas was the least brave and, thus, the most apt to reveal the secret hideout of the Pajama Gang. This being so, she merely waved her wand and dropped an iron cage over him.

And what of Suzy? She heard the cage clang down over Hermit and knew she was next. In desperation, she glanced at the black hole. It was still there, in the middle of the office. Yes, it was still there, quiet and mysterious and unknown. It must lead somewhere but where? Did it lead toward the light of the Liminal Place or toward the darkness of the Undreamt? Phantos had stepped through it, so maybe it was the descent into the underworld. On the other hand, didn't Remmy say that Phantos had closed the gateway to the Liminal Place and hidden it somewhere? Suppose she did so with those magic scissors of hers?

Phantos, from the corner of her dark-painted eyes, saw Suzy take off. She aimed her wand and was about to conjure a pit of quicksand that would swallow the girl, when Suzy leaped through the hole!

She was gone, in an instant.

The dreamworld vanished.

Phantos and Finkel and the mares, caged Hermit and stony Orion and frozen Sky and Ulala, all of them vanished.

The next thing Suzy knew she was yawning, yawning with her head against a pillow and her body sprawled upon a mattress.

It was not her bunkbed at Mount Nightlight, nor was it her creaky twin bed at her aunt and uncle's place. It was a spacious bed, king size, and it was comfy and cushiony and redolent of lavender.

Sunlight trickled in through the gauzy window curtains and shone warmly on Suzy's curly bangs. The sun felt like a gentle hand. It was all tenderness and caress. Birds tweeted from the outside. Sparrows, she guessed, and a pair of blue jays. When Suzy inhaled, the fragrance of blossoms came waltzing into her nose. Suzy smiled contentedly and hugged the sheets to her chin. Oh, the morning was lovely and she wished never to get up!

This silent wish, to sleep forever, tripped an alarm in Suzy's head.

"Sleep? No!" she thought. "Wake! Wake, wake, wake!"

Suzy shot up and threw off the covers. She darted her eyes left and right, her heart going *tap-tap-tap* like a woodpecker drumming a tree.

Where was she? What happened to her friends? To Suzy, the past felt slippery. Like a river stone slickened with algae, it was tricky to grasp and hold onto. She was a Lucid, she was on a quest, she and her friends had gone to Finkel Mansion…and then?

There was a knock at the door. Suzy jerked her head. Two figures, casually dressed, stood in the open doorway. There was a man and a woman.

"Would you look at that," the man whispered to the woman. "Goldilocks has taken our bed."

The woman batted the man's shoulder playfully, then addressed Suzy, saying, "Zuzu, I made you pancakes, and we've got the real maple syrup. Not that artificial junk."

There was only one man in the world who teasingly called her Goldilocks. And there was only one woman in the world who affectionately called her Zuzu.

"*Dad!*" Suzy cried out. "*Mom!*"

CHAPTER THIRTEEN

THE END

Suzy scarfed down seven pancakes that morning. She was all rapture, all endorphins and dopamine. So ecstatic was she to be home again and in the company of her parents, she could have downed another seven. Fortunately for her ballooning stomach, her mother ran out of batter.

Over breakfast Suzy babbled on about her wacky experiences of late, beginning with a wall of graffiti and a curious blue lynx. She told them about the sleep spell and a secret mountain and the children who lived there. She told them about Phantos and her puppet ruler, President Finkel. She told them how they, her parents, had gone off in search of the Liminal Place and never returned.

"Well," she said, as her parents stared at her in silence, "didn't you do that?"

Her mother and father shared a peculiar look. If this look were a recipe, it would be 3/4 cup amusement and 1/4 cup worry, with a dash of pity. Her mother touched her arm. "Zuzu," she said, "your imagination is off the charts."

"What do you mean? I didn't make this up. I couldn't make this up."

Her father remarked, "Maybe not, but your unconscious definitely did."

Her father, a professor of Psychology, was always going on about the unconscious, so Suzy knew exactly what he meant. "You think this was all a dream?" she asked him.

Her mother jumped in. "But, hon, you yourself said it was a dream."

"A dreamworld," Suzy corrected. Her head began to feel fuzzy as she tried to explain the difference. "The dreamworld isn't real, but the world did fall asleep—that really happened!" Her story was capsizing like a leaky ship, she could feel it. She tried a different tack, saying, "Doesn't the name Harold Dore mean anything to you?"

Mr. Schuster simpered at his wife. "Wasn't that an old boyfriend?"

"Oh, please," she scolded him.

Her father became serious again. "Look, Suzy, what's more likely? That the world fell asleep and you befriended a talking blue lynx and a gang of extrasensory children, in a dualistic struggle of truth and light against darkness and illusion…or that you had a bad dream? Remember Occam and his razor? The simplest explanation is usually truest."

Suzy slumped in her seat, feeling foolish and more than a little doubtful. The more she thought about it, the more convincing her father's argument seemed. After all, if her story were true, where was the proof? Where, for instance, were her red bathrobe and flannel pajamas? Where were her flight pillow and bags of sand? Where were her wake mask and the can of Dreamffiti? At present, she had on a plain white nightgown, and the only sand she possessed was to be found in the corners of her eyes.

Suzy got dressed and headed outside. She was baffled, but not the least sad, to see that the ramshackle tenements and the slummy filth and the industrial pollutants that smeared the air like dirty fingerprints were gone.

The sky was blue!

The streets were clean!

The tenements had had their Cinderella moment, transformed to handsome brownstones with cherry trees and firs and leaves of ivy greening their exteriors.

She saw people driving cars, in full control of their destinations and destinies. The only police officer she observed was not wearing body armor. Moreover, his eyes were in plain view, not hidden behind a face shield.

There was an old man, Suzy's neighbor, sweeping his stoop. Suzy cupped her mouth and called to him.

"Excuse me!"

The man leaned on his broom and looked over.

"I only wanted to ask," Suzy went on, "what do you think of Finkel?"

"Finkel who?" replied the man.

"Finkel who!" exclaimed Suzy, loving his response very much. "Finkel who! And what, if you don't mind, does the Unum mean to you?"

The man knitted his brow, then answered, "Not a darn thing."

Suzy spun on her toes, laughing. It was all so wonderful, so miraculous. Maybe it had all been a dream, like her parents said. Maybe her unconscious had contrived the whole episode. In any event, the nightmare was over.

Suzy beheld a group of kids playing kickball in a playground down the road. The playground was open, not closed on account of splinters, and the children were not clothed in funeral-black uniforms but in a variety of colors and styles. She ran over and joined their game and none of them called her "Snoozy Suzy" or poked fun at her. Somehow, they knew her name. After a short while, Suzy remembered theirs too. Heather, Carl, Mikey, and Ella, and they were her friends.

There is an old saying that maintains that the more fun you're having, the faster time flies. It's really not just a saying, but a self-evident truth. For we know that when waiting to see the dentist to have our teeth drilled, the minutes drag their heels, much as we do when finally we are called in. Conversely, holidays and parties and summer breaks never seem to last long enough. So it went with Suzy who, returned to her happy home, caught whiplash from the passing days and weeks. She tore through the pages of her calendar and sprouted inches overnight. No sooner had she turned twelve than a whole year came and went and there she was, blowing out thirteen candles.

She made lifelong friends in middle school. She liked biology, hated chemistry, loved English, and played the drums in band. She received a puppy one Christmas. She fell for this boy, Alexander Kooler, and he asked her to the homecoming dance. She came full bloom into womanhood and could no longer fit into her old clothes and no longer had need of her old toys and old books—the ones with pictures. Her dad now had more hair around his chin and less around his temples and reduced his jogs from 5 miles a day to 2 miles. Her mother put on weight, then lost it, then put it on again, then lost it again, and tried many a diet fad that never stuck. They published papers in various medical and psychiatric journals and always celebrated by raising toasts, and Suzy, when she was old enough, partook of the champagne. Before she knew it, she was buckled into her first car and waving to her parents from the curb. Then came college and new friends and many a mistake and many a righting of said mistakes, and always life seemed as smooth as the surface of a frozen lake.

Then, wedding bells! Alexander Kooler was the groom and everyone that mattered in Suzy's life was present to bear testament to their true love. Her father wept like a baby and Uncle Norman, always practical, held a box of tissues for his convenience. Braydon, now an accomplished vocalist and a very decent young man, performed at the reception with his band called The Reformers, and they all partied until the break of dawn.

Once, when she was a new mother and had a daughter named Angelina, Suzy was lounging on the couch with her watching an animal show on TV. There was a brief segment on a wildcat called a lynx. Suzy blinked hard. Her brainwaves jammed up like a radio. She murmured aloud a peculiar word, a word that meant nothing to her: "Remmy." And her daughter, who was only four and found almost anything silly, repeated this word and sniggered. Suzy laughed too and, chalking the episode up to "mom brain", discarded the incident into the waste bin of time.

Suzy Schuster had, with her husband Alexander, two more children after that and their names were Aurora and Daisy. She opened her own small business, called Snoozy Suzy's?, selling organic mattresses and pillows and other bedding material and it was a resounding success. When she created the marketing tagline, "Pillows so soft, you'll swear you're flying!", she did not, in her wildest imagination, entertain that she had ever flown on winged pillows, up and down mountains and around clouds.

The years, like the pillows, flew.

Her children grew taller and less clumsy. Her parents grew shorter and more clumsy. When her dad died, her mother moved in with them and they sold the brownstone. Suzy's house of five became a house of six. Then the house of six became a house of three when the children fledged and left the nest. Then the house of three became a house of two when Suzy's mother passed away in her sleep, swiftly and quietly, much like the passing of time.

Suzy's children now had families of their own and lives of their own, and the seasons raced each other round the livelong year, like a dog chasing its tail.

Eventually, my friends, eventually we come to the part where our dear Suzy was an old woman. Her golden hair was white now, and her skin creased and worn, though not from frowning and sighing, no, but from smiling in daily abundance. She was a content old thing, spry and witty. Like a campfire subsiding in the night yet still sparking, she became at times very, let us say, *lucid* and dispensed embers of wisdom to her family and friends. She loved to gather her grandchildren about her and counsel them to always apply critical thinking to whatever they did, to practice self-reliance and compassion and to always seek the truth.

"Believe nothing," she would tell them, "without investigating first, and never let fear lead you down the path of tyranny. Hold onto what makes you human, love your neighbor, help those in need, respect the earth, and give thanks for what you have."

The grandchildren agreed: no one talked like Grandma Suzy. She was a rare and special lady, a lady times a thousand!

But all good things, even rare and special ladies, must come to an end. Hear the beep-beep-beep of her cardiograph machine. See the pale woman lying supine on the hospital bed, wheezing through an oxygen mask.

The room in which she lay was sterile, lacking warmth and color. There was a row of windows and Suzy wished the nurse would raise the blinds, but the other patient—a sleepy old man—had complained that the sun bothered his cataracts. Suzy's daughters and grandchildren had just left. They visited her every day and were, she reflected, sweet and caring but would probably rather be doing something else. This was hard for them, she knew. To watch a loved one slowly fade away and be unable to help. This was hard, indeed.

The nurse walked in, uniformed in green scrubs. Suzy wished the nurse, just this once, would wear a dress or a sweater or, heck, even a pair of pajamas, anything but that yucky green uniform. The nurse offered Suzy food, and for the first time since her admission to the hospital, Suzy declined the tray. She would have eaten if she had the appetite, but today, she knew, today it was not happening. Today might be it. In pity, the nurse motioned to the screen on the wall and asked whether she would like to watch a show. Suzy waved her frail, liver-spotted hand—she meant "no," but the nurse, misunderstanding, turned on the TV anyway.

"Oh, well," thought Suzy. "What does it matter now? And, who knows, maybe the tube will distract me from the pain. If there will be any."

Suzy hoped the end would be easy, as frictionless as the rest of her life. "It was a long life," she reflected, "but too short. Everything went by so terribly fast."

The beeping of the cardiograph slowed. *Beep... beep...beep.* And over this sound came laughter. The laugh track of a sitcom, the one on TV. Suzy squinted at the actors and actresses on screen. She tried to piece together what was happening. There was a family. OK. There was a collie. Fine. And there was a girl in the hall closet, on her knees, rummaging for something or other and saying, "Dad, the dog did it again!"

On the screen, an overweight man in a flannel shirt and jeans appeared and said, "Did what, honey bunny?"

"Took my shoe!" cried the girl. "I'm missing a shoe!"

The dad held up a chewed-up, spat-out sneaker and said, "It's not exactly missing, though parts of it are."

The laugh track again, filling the long intervals between the beats of Suzy's heart.

"Oh, great," moaned the girl, throwing up her arms. "Guess I gotta bunny-hop to school then."

"Not necessarily," said the dad, tossing the sneaker back to the dog. "You could kangaroo jump or frog leap."

Something about this plotline caused Suzy's eyelids to crack open a full half-inch wider than they had in many years. She leaned forward. She stretched her neck. She wriggled her lips. A voice inside her whispered: *That was me.*

The beeps of the cardiograph began to pick up. Fast.

That was me.

In her head, a flashlight flicked on and illuminated the dim and dusty corners where she had stashed away Orion, Hermit, Sky, and Remmy.

I was missing a shoe, a turquoise shoe with white laces, and it was the last thing my parents gave me before they left to find the...the...the...

At the top of her lungs, which were not very powerful, she croaked, "Liminal Place!"

Hearing her outburst, the sleepy old man who shared the room with her hollered at her that she was liable to wake the dead, which wasn't far off the mark.

Suzy removed her bedsheet and stared at her feet. The long white socks covering her veiny feet seemed wrong. False. She squinted and concentrated, trying to see the truth of what was really there. Her eyes pinched close, then reopened. And, lo, there on her right foot was a shabby old shoe.

"My shoe!" she sang out. "My shoe, it's still there! All this time!"

The sleepy old man began harping again, but no matter. Suzy was already up and hobbling out of the room. Her feeble heart cried, "Stop!" Her wheezing lungs shouted, "Don't!" Her brittle bones demanded, "Go back! Go back!" The body of the aged said one thing; the soul of the youth said another. Suzy pressed on. Doctors, patients, visitors, nurses, and residents gaped at her as though she had risen from the dead. Not a few of them exhorted her to return to her bed. They called her weak and sickly and said she was liable to hurt herself.

"I am not weak," Suzy told herself, puffing along. "I'm not this crone you see; I am eleven! I am a girl, a girl searching for her lost shoe, for her parents, for the lost world of Reality and Truth!"

Invigorated by these thoughts, Suzy felt old age releasing her from its grip. Her gait quickened, her spine straightened, her stride increased. Had she a mirror to view herself, she would have seen her wrinkles vanishing and her skin tightening. Meanwhile, in her chest, there was a magnificent rejuvenation, with her breaths becoming deep and her heartbeats becoming strong. By the time she had reached the front desk, she was barely recognizable as the centenarian she once was. She looked not a day over 50. It was a wonder that her nurse could even identify her, but she did.

"Now just where in the name of Lazarus do you think you're going, Mrs. Kooler?" she exclaimed, cutting in front of Suzy.

"That's not my name!" shouted Suzy and shoved the woman aside.

The nurse cried for help. Hurrying toward the exit doors, Suzy heard footsteps behind her. She glanced over her shoulder and beheld three men with stars pinned to their khaki shirts barreling toward her.

Hospital security.

She began to run.

And as she ran, the years dropped away from her. One second, she was a slowpoke forty-year-old; the next second, a modestly fast thirty-year-old; now, suddenly, she was a twenty-something with the lung capacity of a triathlete! Nearing the exit, she shed her womanhood entirely and reduced a full foot in height. She was a child again, with bright blue eyes and curly gold hair and a lovely bathrobe of scarlet.

The exit doors, when she tried to shove them open, refused to budge, for they had been remotely locked. Suzy, wise now to the illusions that had held her captive for almost an entire century, rebuked the doors with a defiant scream and shattered them to pieces.

With a bound, she was free of the hospital.

Immediately there was an explosive boom.

The ground shook seismically.

Whirling around, Suzy witnessed the hospital crumbling to the ground—crumbling as if from a demolition! She ducked down and clapped her ears as a howling wind washed over her, carrying dust and debris and ghostly moans from a life that never was.

CHAPTER FOURTEEN

RETURN TO
MOUNT NIGHTLIGHT

Even before the dust cloud settled, even blinded, Suzy knew where she was.

She was in the Undreamt, and she had almost died.

If she had died, and praise be she did not, the epitaph on her tombstone might have read: "Killed by a hoax," or perhaps, "Fooled to death." For, truly, no one attacked her; no one poisoned or starved her. She had merely grown quite ancient, or presumed she had grown so, and believed that her time had come.

"Maybe," Suzy thought with a shiver, "that was how Phantos got you." She or he or whatever it was webbed you in a dream, a dream so delightful, so pleasurable and perfect, that you became complicit in it. You stayed in the dream because you wished to, because you enjoyed it. And when you died in the dream you did so willingly, with peace and satisfaction.

Oh, it was a grand deception!

Suzy was so shaken by the whole experience, she examined her hands several times, searching for wrinkles, blotches, veins, and other dermatological evidence of old age. Convinced at last that she was young again, Suzy turned her eyes outward.

She was standing on a plain of obsidian rock. The ground was black, shiny, and hard. Streams of lava flowed in every direction, while geysers exploded from the ground and erected towers of fire that flashed like lightning before splashing down into molten pools.

The air was suffocating. When Suzy inhaled, her throat burned. It was like sticking your head next to a puffing chimney and trying to breathe.

Somehow, on this fire-fed land, there grew stands of trees. But these were of a type wholly unknown to our green world, for their branches were as red as capillaries and as sinuous as the tentacles of a giant squid. They bore no leaves but did boast of fruit, these being blood-red apples festering with worms.

Finally, to complete her survey, Suzy peered at the sky. There was no sun, no moon, no stars or planets, only a thick ceiling of smoke. In one direction, below the layer of smoke, floated an enormous pyramid. The floating pyramid was made of the same black volcanic rock as the rest of the land. And flapping batlike around this pyramid, as though it were their hive or nest, were innumerable creatures with horns and tails.

"Mares," Suzy murmured to herself.

Dreading that one of these monsters might spot her and come swooping at her with their claws outstretched, she sheltered under the nearest tree. She hoped the tree's bizarre branches would conceal her. In fact, as we shall see, the tree did the very opposite.

First, the tree dropped an apple at her feet. Had Suzy been as naïve as Snow White, she might have picked it up and gobbled it down. But, plainly, one did not eat rotten apples from a tentacled tree rooted in molten fire. She kicked it away. The tree responded to this act of ingratitude by coiling its tentacles around her ankles, her shins, her waist and arms. Caught in these branches, which were stickier than chewing gum, the tree heaved her into the air.

"Let me down!" Suzy shouted to the tree. "Let go! Let me go!"

She writhed to no avail. The tree passed her higher and higher, up through its canopy, until she was at the very crown and wholly exposed to the mares in the sky.

Then, from somewhere, a stern voice called out: "Release her, Grabapple Tree!"

The Grabapple Tree whimpered like a scolded dog. Then it lowered Suzy to the ground. Its tentacles uncoiled from around her body and slithered back to the trunk like serpents.

Free of the grasping tree, Suzy beheld a figure advancing toward her. She couldn't make out who it was, for the atmosphere of the Undreamt was so very dim and smoky. But when the figure was ten paces away, a geyser of lava erupted from a crater and by its light Suzy beheld the face of the stranger.

It was a homely face, yet a human face, and thus it ought to have been a welcome face, were it not that the face belonged to Harold Dore.

"What do you want from me?" Suzy demanded of him. She was ready to defend herself if necessary, and demonstrated her readiness by clasping one of the green bags on her sash.

The gangly young man in the black T-shirt and jeans looked frightened, though not of Suzy. He kept glancing at the mares, while beads of sweat stuck to his forehead.

"How did you do it?" he muttered, scarcely above a whisper. "How did you dissolve the doubledream?"

Suzy was about to inquire what a doubledream was, when Harold, who spoke as though he had a ticking bomb strapped to his chest, hurried on breathlessly: "The prisons of the Undreamt are not made of mortar and brick, but dreams—dreams within dreams, doubledreams. They are where dissidents like yourself end up and where they die. Only you outsmarted it, didn't you?"

Suzy replied, tersely, that she supposed she did. "How long was I in there for?" she asked him. She worried that 89 years had gone by, which would mean that all her friends at Mount Nightlight would be either in, or near, the grave.

"In dream time, a day," answered Harold. "In real-world time, which goes much, much slower, maybe two seconds."

"That would mean," began Suzy, trying to do the math in her head. But Harold interrupted, saying, "Twelve minutes in Reality is a year in the Dreamworld. Which means you and the rest of humanity have been asleep for less than one hour."

Suzy was greatly relieved to hear this. It was a tremendous consolation to know that people were not dreaming their lives away and that, if and when the spell broke, everyone would awaken from what amounted to a catnap.

Harold stepped toward her. "You and I are a lot alike," he went on. "Back in Reality, among all those landlubbers, we were lonely fish, craving the fluid medium of dream. And look at us now!" He chuckled, his bony shoulders bobbing up and down. It was the weirdest laugh Suzy had ever witnessed. There was exultation in it and misery, the damaged pride of the gambler who has won the world but lost his soul.

"We aren't at all alike," Suzy insisted. "I never would have partnered with a monster."

At the mention of Phantos, Harold flinched and scanned the sky with utmost caution. Then, resuming, he spoke more rapidly than before: "It is my failing, yes. I own it, I accept it, I blame no one but myself. I aligned with a demon who promised me ultimate power and became the public face of an evil authority. You asked me what I want, so I'll tell you: what I want is what you want, what I seek is what you seek. To be perfectly clear, I wish my dream to end and the world to awaken!"

Suzy was incredulous. Having been fooled so many times, she was more than inclined to doubt him. Why would the man behind the Unum wish to overthrow the Unum? It made no sense. But then Suzy recalled something she had stored in the back of her mind—namely, how Harold, speaking as Finkel to the demon Phantos, in the supposed privacy of his presidential office, had expressed a desire to uplift the people, to enrich and empower them and better their lives.

"You betrayed my parents," Suzy told him. "You tricked the world and made life awful for so very many. But if you mean what you say, help me: show me the way to the Liminal Place!"

Harold shook his head. "I can't do that," he replied. "No one can. Don't you get it by now? The twilight people won't wake up until they wise up, until they see through the lies and illusions of this magic mirror! There's no shortcut to the Liminal Place. No hidden door. No hack. The portal will only appear once awareness is achieved. That's it."

Suzy thought of Uncle Norman and Aunt Millie. She thought of Ms. Canary, Principal Winslow, and the Red Suits. She thought of the great multitude of sleepwalkers and became immediately depressed.

"That will never happen," she said.

"I wish I could disagree," said Harold.

His frown was the same as Suzy's, and they held their frowns together for a whole minute. Then Harold said, "You should go."

He reached into the back pocket of his jeans and fetched a pair of golden scissors—the same marvelous pair he had used back at Finkel Mansion. Harold got to work at once. His blades snipped the hot, hazy air and very soon there was another black hole. "This will take you back to the mountain," he told her, when he was done cutting.

Suzy shot him a worried look. Did he just say mountain? How did he know about Mount Nightlight?

"What have you done?" she asked with trepidation.

Harold averted his gaze from Suzy's. He looked suddenly ill, feverish, sick to his stomach. "There was nothing I could do," he mumbled. For emphasis he repeated this statement, but with such a guilty expression that a jury would have convicted him on the spot.

"What happened?" Suzy implored. "What happened to my friends?"

"You'll see," Harold said darkly. He motioned to the hole, saying, "We've wasted enough time. Go now, before the mares see you."

Suzy approached the hole, then thought of something and spun back to Harold. She dug into her bathrobe pocket, produced the can of Dreamffiti, and held it out to him. He hesitated, staring dumbly at the gift she was offering him. Suzy explained: "It's kind of like a phone...but with paint. I was thinking we might keep in touch. Maybe we can help each other."

She lifted her big blue eyes to his somber face, and with such goodwill and fellowship that he was struck speechless. Probably he had met few people in his life as kind and forgiving as the girl. It was also probably the case that he had partaken of the poisonous grin of Phantos so often, that Suzy's bright smile was like antivenom for his soul. He took the can from her and hurried away.

Once more, Suzy faced the black hole. She hefted one leg through it, then the other. She stumbled forward in the darkness. A second later, she blinked her eyes and found herself in a forest clearing.

It was day and, like almost every day in the Unum, overcast and gray. A bitter fog pervaded the woodland, its ghostly tendrils reaching among the withered bushes. The forest was scarcely livable. Stunted or fallen trees met Suzy's gaze at every turn. The oak trees were rotting and infested with fungus. The fir trees were dying and losing needles by the hour. There were no animals to be seen, except a bald, one-eyed crow which screeched at her from the naked bough of one of those sickly firs.

"Hush, you old grouch!" Suzy scolded the crow. She was busy thinking, you see, trying to determine in which direction Mount Nightlight lay. She tilted her head, searching for the summit of the mountain. Yet, for some odd reason, she could not find it.

Then she heard a most unnatural forest sound. It came from the sky. The sound went like this: *Thwop-thwop-thwop-thwop-thwop!*

The sound grew louder and louder and eventually became so overpowering that even the one-eyed crow held his peace and listened.

Then Suzy looked up and saw them. The helicopters passed directly overhead. She had no idea what a flock of helicopters is called, but they resembled a flock of crows—great big crows with machineguns—and so she called them "a murder." The murder of helicopters *thwop-thwop-thwopped* across the sky, vanishing toward the horizon. With a feeling of cold dread, Suzy ran off in the direction they had come from.

She had covered about a mile when, abruptly, she stumbled upon the mountain. It was obvious to her now why she had failed to see it before. For the awesome summit, formerly at the top of the mountain where it belonged, was now buried in the ground like an upside-down pyramid.

The mountain had lost half its height, but that was not all. The part that remained had been blown open, like a clamshell cracked in two. The secret hollows and winding tunnels were laid bare. That exhilarating rollercoaster, *The R.E.M. Express*, was scattered in pieces and its steel track all twisted and gnarled. The bunkbeds on which the Lucids slept were now charred and smoldering, reduced to firewood.

Mount Nightlight, Suzy realized as a pang struck her heart, was no more.

But a still greater fear gripped her. After all, a mountain is just a lot of stone; it was the people who lived there, who played and learned and laughed there, that made it special. And where were they?

Suzy scoured the ruins for her fellow Lucids. She called out their names. She called out a hundred names, all the ones she could remember, before her voice grew hoarse and she abandoned the effort. There were no Lucids left. No Nyxies either.

All was not lost, however. There was still one hope—one whiskery hope, furred and fearless and wise.

She began to look for him right away. She searched high and low. She combed over the stones with more care and attention than an archeologist. She yodeled his name into the blasted hollows of the mountain. She climbed, she descended, she peeked and prodded and wandered, until returning to the base of the toppled summit she gazed up at it and beheld something orange fluttering in the wind.

"Remmy!" she screamed in relief. "Remmy!"

The escarpment was too steep to climb, so Suzy unbuckled the pillow from her back and flew instead. But when she reached the top of the inverted summit and hopped off her pillow, she saw that while the bathrobe remained, the lynx was gone. The saffron robe, draped over a stone and stirring in the breeze, was shredded. Little blur hairs lay scattered everywhere about. There must have been a struggle, a fierce and terrible battle, the outcome of which was apparent in the razed mountain and in her missing friends and in the tattered robe of her teacher.

The lightbearers had lost.

Suzy dropped to her knees. She buried her face in her hands. Her tears fell and her hope died. And in the distance, somewhere in that dying forest, a one-eyed crow laughed and laughed.

CHAPTER FIFTEEN

THE SAND VAULT

Remulus, by all appearances, was out of the picture. Either he had been killed, or he had been dragged to the Undreamt and made a prisoner. Suzy, who herself had served time in the Undreamt and experienced its ghastly fires and grabbing trees, to say nothing of its doubledreams, could not decide which fate was worse.

How long Suzy would have remained on her knees, covering her face in despair, we may only speculate. Whether she would have mourned fifteen hours or fifteen days, it is impossible to estimate, because after about fifteen minutes a faint scuffing noise, as of bath slippers on stone, distracted her.

Suzy glanced over her shoulder. Halfway across the mesa-like rock, which was as long as a city block, there appeared a girl with a pillow tucked under her arm.

Suzy ran to her.

"Sky!" cried Suzy, hugging and squeezing her and pecking her cheek. "You melted! You're all right! You unfroze! You're here! You're really here!"

Suzy was ecstatic, and with good reason. The last time they were together Sky hadn't a pulse. Suzy recalled only too vividly how her friend had looked, trapped in a sheet of ice, pale and blue-lipped, her mouth frozen in a silent scream. In similar fashion, Phantos had fixed Orion in stone and Hermit in a cage. Thinking of the boys, Suzy asked: "Is anyone else left?"

Sky had not reciprocated anything from Suzy thus far: not her hug, not her kiss, not her euphoria. And she remained cold and uncommunicative even now, by glumly shaking her head. Her hair was still blue and her kimono still a plummy purple. But, otherwise, the girl hardly resembled Suzy's intrepid bunkmate. Suzy wondered whether Sky had thawed all the way through or was perhaps still chilly in the middle, like Aunt Millie's potpies.

"What's wrong?" Suzy asked her.

"Everything," came Sky's truthful reply. "And it's all my fault."

"Not at all," Suzy argued. "We did what we could. No one's to blame for what happened. We tried. We tried, Sky. That's got to be worth something!"

Dropping her pillow, Sky grabbed Suzy by her bathrobe and shook her violently. "I did this! Me! I told Phantos, I told Phantos about Mount Nightlight! I led them here—the soldiers, the generals, Phantos too! Remmy tried to protect us—he gave himself over, he surrendered under the condition that us Lucids be spared, but Phantos double-crossed him and captured every last one of us—except me! She left me because I'm the traitor! She should've taken me, but she didn't!"

Suzy was dumbfounded. Naturally, she had assumed that it would have been timid Hermit who broke first and volunteered information to Phantos. That it was Sky baffled her.

Sky must have picked up on Suzy's confusion or else felt compelled to explain herself, for she went on, saying, "I tried to tell you. I told you I didn't want to go back. I didn't want Wakesville. Yeah, it's clean and sweet and free and all that, but my parents aren't there, are they? Nothing will ever change that. But here—here, at least— I had Remmy and all you. Phantos…she convinced me I was doing the right thing. She promised me that none of my friends would be harmed. She said she would only take Remmy, and I, uh…"

Sky flinched in memory of the betrayal. Flinched as though Remmy had raised his paw to swat her a deserving blow, which, of course, he would never have done.

"It's all right," Suzy coaxed. "If you didn't talk, Phantos would have made Hermit talk or Orion."

"Wrong!" shouted Sky. "Phantos tried with them and they refused! They were strong! They were loyal! I was weak!"

"I don't blame you."

"Yeah, well, I do!"

"You're my friend," Suzy said gently. "We need each other, now more than ever."

"There's nothing left," said Sky, staring in misery at the ruins of Mount Nightlight.

"What about our friends," Suzy pleaded. "The Lucids. What about them?"

"I'm not one of you anymore." Sky removed her gold sash tied with velvet bags and dumped it on the ground. "I don't deserve to be."

Sky shifted her teary gaze from Suzy to what lay beyond Suzy—namely, the precipice. She stared at the edge and smiled most peculiarly.

"You were always better than me, Snoozy," said Sky, still smiling that weird smile. "You did things no one else could, like flying without a pillow. But, hey, maybe this time, I'll show you up. And, if not, deep sleep ain't so bad. I'll wake up…someday."

By the time Suzy grasped her meaning, Sky had already shoved her out of the way and bolted toward the edge of the rock.

"Sky!" Suzy cried in dread.

She chased after Sky, but she wasn't as fast and Sky reached the precipice a few steps before she did. Sky dove into the air and fell. Suzy, having no recourse to her flight pillow, which she had left near the tatters of Remmy's robe, jumped after her.

It was a terrifying sight: two girls plunging from the top of what amounted to a small mountain, with no trampoline or safety net under them and no bungy cords or parachutes on their backs.

Sky shut her eyes in terror. Suzy kept her eyelids peeled, if only so that she might not lose sight of the friend she must save.

And, as her eyes were open, Suzy beheld that directly under them, at the base of this enormous mesa and coming on fast, was a wide chasm in the ground. Sky penetrated it first, screaming her head off, whereat Suzy followed next, with a scream to match.

The two girls sank through the abyss, which grew darker as the surface receded behind them. The chasm was so dark and empty, and the girls felt so weightless in freefall, it might have been outer space. Or a coal mine. Or an elevator shaft. Or the chute of an impossible dumbwaiter. Or the subterranean launch station of an evil supervillain's nuclear missiles.

To tell the truth, the girls had no idea.

Now, as everyone has a bottom, it stands to reason that every object does too. The chasm had a bottom, and it appeared as a sparkle, a shimmer, a bright glittery ground. And it was thanks to this sparkly light that Suzy could see her friend. Suzy straightened her limbs—a pencil dive—and, by this, managed to accelerate herself and catch up to Sky. She wrapped Sky in her arms and cried, "I got you!" Sky held onto Suzy as tightly as the latter held onto her.

Suzy thought in a flash—for when one is falling at terminal velocity, one can only think in flashes—of how Hermit had squeezed her hand when she first entered Mount Nightlight. How he had made her feel welcome and safe through this one tender gesture. How much stronger, Suzy thought, is a person when he or she is united, at the very flesh, to another! Her mind flashed forth truths that were plain and undeniable: Distance divides! Division destroys! But love and togetherness uplift!

Similar realizations were bursting through Sky's head just then.

Locked in each other's embrace, both girls knew what to say and with one voice exclaimed, "Just a dream!"

At this utterance, they halted. They floated about 18 1/2 inches from the ground. Then, as gently as leaves riding an autumn wind, they lowered 18 1/2 inches and settled onto a sandy surface.

It was like a beach—a magical beach with snow-cone dunes of red sand, green sand, blue sand, yellow sand, orange sand, violet sand, and more! The sand sparkled like rubies and emeralds and amethysts. It gave off its own magnificent light, and a good thing too, or else the girls wouldn't have been able to see a thing, being as they were several miles underground.

Suzy and Sky shared a look of astonishment.

"Dreamsand," murmured Suzy.

"Dreamsand," murmured Sky.

Their murmurs returned to them in echoes.

"What is this place?" asked Suzy. She spoke quietly, reverently, as if she were in a temple or holy shrine, and well she might have been.

"There were always rumors about where Remmy kept his sand," said Sky. "You know Nightcap?"

"The boy who wears the nightcap?" Suzy ventured, with sound logic.

"Him. He was always saying the sand was under the mountain, in a hidden vault. A sand vault. Guess we found it."

Suzy, rousing herself from her awed stupor, began to stroll through the vault. Sky hurried after her.

"Careful!" said Sky, motioning to a heap of green braingrains. "I'd steer clear of that stuff."

"For sure," replied Suzy.

They wandered among the dunes. It was like being in an art museum, and every now and then they paused to appreciate the brilliancy of a certain sand or to remark, like afficionados, on its particular effect. The stone vault was enormous—miles long, miles wide, and seemingly without end. But the longer they toured the vault, the guiltier Sky became. The sand reminded her of her teacher. Which reminded her of her betrayal. Which reminded her of how forgiving and understanding Suzy had been.

"Thank you," she cried, hugging Suzy with the strength of a young lion. "You were right; we need each other."

Sky pulled away and dried her eyes and assumed her usual look, which was rather serious and determined. "Maybe we can still do it, Snoozy. You and I, we can find the Liminal Place together!"

Then Suzy told her what Harold Dore had told her, namely, that the Liminal Place was not to be found but earned. And it could only be earned once the multitudes realized that their world was an illusion, a shadow play run by shadowy demons. The hearts and minds of the people had to radically change, to evolve, or they would be forever stuck in the dream.

"But that'll never happen," moaned Sky, which, if you recall, were Suzy's sentiments exactly.

"I wish I could disagree," sighed Suzy, which, if you recall, were Harold Dore's sentiments exactly.

"If only we could put these grains to some use," said Sky, gazing round at the dunes. Her eyes fell upon an impressive mound of green sand. Something tickled her about this, and she snorted a laugh. "Can you imagine if that goofball Orion were here? He'd scoop up all those braingrains and shower the whole world with 'em!"

But Suzy did not find this funny. Not at all. Something about the whimsical image of Orion sprinkling braingrains over the people of the Unum struck her not as comical but inspiring.

"Not braingrains," Suzy said thoughtfully.

"Say what?" asked Sky.

"That's the wrong kind," Suzy added, and away she ran.

Suzy retraced her steps toward the vast chasm through which they had fallen. Not far from there could be found a very unique sand. Remmy had called it "soul sand," and it was diamond-shiny and diamond-clear. Suzy, exploring a little, discovered heaps of it—hills and ridges and powdery ski-slopes of it, all amassed in rows that twinkled as far as the eye could see. The finest jewelry store in the world was nothing compared to its splendor.

As rich as the soul sand was to behold, how much richer was it to experience! Suzy had not forgotten, nor probably ever would, her Lighting Ceremony and how Remmy had smeared her forehead with it and, in doing so, opened her mind like a coconut shell. Her soul had flown away and visited that mass transit system between Dream and Reality known as the Liminal Place. Suzy mused aloud: "If the sand helped me see the truth, then it should help the twilight people do the same!"

Sky came upon her, whereat Suzy revealed her plan. Sky, who had also been touched with soul sand during her own Lighting Ceremony, acknowledged that such sand might nudge the sleepwalkers in the right direction. Yet, being more practical than Suzy, she pointed out the humungous hurdle their plan would face: "How we gonna get all that sand to all those people?"

They were but two girls and the sleepwalkers numbered in the billions. Suzy and Sky might be able to toss sand from their flight pillows, but they could hardly expect to reach more than a few hundred people. And a few hundred people was not enough. Not even close. Their mentor and their friends were in the hands of the enemy. Whatever Suzy and Sky did, it had to be done fast and on a massive scale.

They were silent for a while—the way people get when they've hit a wall and have no further ideas. Sky suggested, half ironically, that they sleep on it. She was very tired, what with her emotional rollercoaster from guilt and self-loathing to love and self-forgiveness. Suzy, who a short while ago believed she was an elderly woman on the cusp of death, was also a tad drained.

"Let's rest here for the night," Suzy suggested, peering overhead at the dark chasm where not even the faintest ray of daylight could be observed. "Tomorrow we'll start over fresh."

"Sounds like a plan," said Sky.

But, being Lucids, the girls could not deceive themselves so easily. They knew it was not a plan. It was a deferment of making a plan, which they had been utterly unable to do. It was not a good feeling to have, and they curled up on the sandy floor that night with heavy hearts and worried minds.

CHAPTER SIXTEEN

BRING IN THE AVIATORS!

It was near midnight when Suzy, who was too troubled for sleep, heard a voice.

"Are you there?" asked the voice. "Can you hear me?"

Suzy sat up, shook the sand from her yellow hair, and listened.

"Answer me, please!" the voice pleaded.

Strangely, the voice seemed close at hand—if not at her elbow than in her ear. Nonetheless, Suzy could plainly see there was no one around except Sky, who lay asleep beside her.

"This is a waste," grumbled the voice. "I knew it wouldn't work. Can of paint? Yeah, right!"

It was the mention of paint that allowed Suzy to connect the dots. The jaded voice. The can of Dreamffiti. Why, it was Harold Dore, of course!

Suzy scrambled onto her feet, and not knowing what would happen, she cried, "Wait!"

"Suzy?" said Harold.

"Yes," she answered.

"Hang on," replied the disembodied voice. "I think— yes, yes—I see you! You're in some kind of sandpit, am I right?"

"Sand vault," Suzy corrected.

Harold cried out, "Brilliant! Then it works! Amazing stuff, kid! Now turn to your right—keep going—now stop! There, now I can see you better."

"But I can't see you," said Suzy. "Where are you?"

Harold was in Finkel Mansion, locked inside his bathroom, completely alone except for the cartoonish- looking girl whom he had painted on his wall. He hadn't actually painted Suzy like, say, an artist paints a vase. He had merely shaken the can and pressed the nozzle and the Dreamffiti had done the rest. He explained all of this to Suzy, however he neglected to mention that he was wearing a nightshirt and pajama pants. His omission was unfortunate, because had Suzy known that her former enemy was not only using Dreamffiti but sporting jammies too, she would have giggled in delight.

"Listen," said Harold. "By now you should understand the danger your friends are in. They're alive, but for how much longer I can't say. They're being held in New Shiny City, at the 99th Precinct. At noon tomorrow, Commissioner Sikman will march them through the streets to the gates of Finkel Mansion, where Finkel will denounce them on live television. They will be made an example of and sentenced to prison for the rest of their lives. Only their prison will be the Undreamt and their cells, doubledreams. They will die there, Suzy. Bet your pillow."

"Then don't do it!" Suzy begged him. "*You* are President Finkel! Don't sentence them! Pardon them!

Release them! You're the leader of this world, it's your dream, do what's right, help your people, help the human race!"

For all her pleading and all her passion, Suzy received no reply. She wondered if Harold had gone away or if the magic of the Dreamffiti had run out. In truth, Harold had silenced himself and become stock-still. For he fancied he had heard the snip, snip, snip of scissors and feared that Phantos was paying him a midnight visit, as the demon often did. He held his breath and listened, only to conclude that his mind was playing tricks.

"That won't be possible," he resumed at last, turning back to the animated version of Suzy on his bathroom wall. "Phantos has forbidden me to take part in tomorrow's operation. She thinks I'm too sympathetic toward my own kind, and so I am. Well, then, tomorrow, Phantos will be President Finkel. The demon will condemn the Pajama Gang—without mercy, you can be sure."

Suzy was so engrossed in her conversation with Harold that she didn't notice Sky creeping up behind her. Sky yawned and blinked her eyes, then mumbled to Suzy: "I thought you said you didn't talk in your sleep?"

"I'm not," replied Suzy. "I'm talking to Finkel. I mean, Harold. Harold Dore."

Sky gave Suzy a look that implied she might benefit from a psychiatric evaluation.

"It's the Dreamffiti," Suzy explained. "I gave Harold a can and…"

"You did what?" Sky exploded.

"He spray-painted me, just like how I painted Remmy when I needed him."

"Oh, terrific," Sky returned sarcastically.

Suzy informed her of the dire situation confronting their fellow Lucids. Now, unlike Suzy, Sky had little room in her heart for forgiving Harold Dore, and, therefore, she lashed out at him, who was not physically there, and dealt him the harshest verbal beatdown she had ever given anyone in her life. After several minutes of this tirade, Harold cut her off, saying, "Alright, alright! I'm worse than a backed-up toilet, I get it! Denounce me all you want, but it won't change anything. Your friends are in danger, and I want to help."

Sky folded her arms and retorted, "Yeah, right! I'd trust a horned viper over President Finkel-Faker." Then, after she had stewed for a bit longer, she inquired of Harold how he intended to help.

"I am," began Harold, "for the little time remaining, still President. As such, I can provide you with virtually anything: money, lawyers, senators, tanks, jets, whatever you need, name it and I'll do it."

All at once, the solution burst upon Suzy. In one galvanizing instant the electrical circuit inside her head completed its loop and a bulb flashed on. "Jets!" she whooped. "Give us your jets! And your pilots! Bring in the aviators!"

"And," ventured Harold, "missiles?"

"No!" cried Suzy, appalled at his suggestion. "Sand! Lots and lots of sand!"

The rest, as they say, was history. The plan was ironed out and everyone, including Harold Dore, loved the idea and was eager to execute it. Soul sand was completely foreign to Harold, yet he trusted the girls and well knew that the Dream Guard possessed magical totems. There wasn't enough soul sand to cover every city in the Unum; not even close. But there was enough to blanket New Shiny City, and that, they all agreed, would be a start. If one city—the capital, no less—woke up, other cities might follow.

As soon as Harold was done scrubbing the Dreamffiti off his wall (he feared Phantos might see it), he transformed into the tall, tan, can-do leader of the world, President Art Q. Finkel. From his bedroom, Finkel hastened to his office—the one with the mare statues and dressing mirror and checkered floor—and phoned a five-starred general of the Unum Air Force (UAF) named Kurt Lovelakes.

General Lovelakes was human. And, so, when his cell phone rang at 3 in the morning, he was not up pacing his room and dreaming up evil schemes like a mare would have been. He was tucked in bed and dreaming, period.

Immediately upon hearing the husky voice on the other line, General Lovelakes rolled out of bed in his underwear and saluted his Commander in Chief as if the latter were standing by the dresser.

"I have a special job for you, General," said President Finkel and proceeded to dictate what needed to be done.

General Lovelakes was incredulous. The aircrafts that Finkel was requesting were used exclusively for spraying the skies, night and day, with toxic metals. It was the chief reason the sky was never blue anymore, but everywhere a leaden gray. "You want our boys to spray…sand?"

Finkel said that he did, and in a tone that was peremptory and final.

"Copy, sir. I'll be at the base in 0400 hours. Goodbye, sir." And, once again, the half-naked general saluted his dresser.

A few hours later, Suzy and Sky heard a commotion overhead. From the surface of the earth came the roar of jets and the whir of helicopters. Then a score of UAF officers in khaki fatigues and with shovels strapped to their backs rappelled into the chasm. They met Suzy and Sky, who directed them to the soul sand.

The airmen marveled at the huge white dunes. One remarked that they reminded him of the pearls his mother used to wear. Another swore that, while staring at the sand, she harked the enchanting music of some bygone instrument (it was a harp). A third began to weep, though he could not explain why. Suzy and Sky, however, required no explanation. They understood what was happening. The soldiers, being so near the sand, felt their souls stirring.

More airmen descended into the vault, and more after that. They wasted no time but shoveled the gleaming sand into a huge steel container. The container was connected by long cables to a helicopter perched aboveground. Once the container was brimming with sand, an airman radioed to the helicopter pilot, shouting, "Heave ho, pilot!" Then the helicopter lifted into the air and brought the container to the surface.

The soldiers had scarcely mopped the sweat from their brows when an empty container, of the same type as the first, was lowered into the vault and the process repeated.

The airmen labored all that morning. They shoveled and sang like happy dwarves and never, not once, complained. Suzy and Sky requested shovels and were given them and did their part too. Container after container of sand reached the surface.

And what, you ask, was happening way up there aboveground? A labor just as backbreaking as that occurring below, I can assure you. Airmen, equipped with spades and standing inside the containers, scooped the sand out and packed it into canisters. These canisters were then fitted onto the wings of military jets, four canisters to a wing.

Now, the ruins of Mount Nightlight were not exactly an ideal runway; in fact, with the rough woodland and copious boulders, it was downright dangerous. There was just enough clear, level land to accommodate one of these planes. So, every time a jet received its grainy payload, it departed and returned to a nearby airbase, whereat another plane descended to be filled.

When the bulk of the soul sand had been withdrawn from the vault, Suzy and Sky threw down their shovels. Their work underground was over; their work aboveground was about to begin. They had their friends to rescue, and both girls knew that this would be the hardest, scariest, most daunting thing they had ever attempted.

The girls got out of the vault the same way the sand did, by riding in a steel container. It felt like a carnival ride, almost as good as *The R.E.M. Express.* When they reached the surface, one of the pilots graciously offered to give the girls a lift to New Shiny City, if such was their destination. But Suzy and Sky politely refused. They had their own wings, thank you very much. Then, to the sheer bewilderment of the airmen, who presumed they had encountered every aircraft under the sun, the girls stepped onto their pillows and flew away.

CHAPTER SEVENTEEN

THE PAJAMA CHAIN GANG

It was an ordinary Sunday in New Shiny City. The smog was dismal, the sun was murky, the streets were as empty as the tenement homes were overcrowded.

These last two conditions, however, were about to reverse: soon the people would begin coming out of doors, and the tenements would be deserted. That is because, just then, an emergency broadcast flickered onto everyone's TVs, tablets, and phones and presented live video of President Art Q. Finkel. Dressed smartly in a suit and tie and seated at his desk, he looked straight into the camera and did what he was indisputably the best at: he lied his pants off.

To his "safe and loyal citizens," President Finkel announced that the Pajama Gang had been arrested. In triumph, he declared victory over the "pillow-toting terrorists" who had recently infiltrated Finkel Mansion and tried to kidnap him. (This ingenious propaganda was the invention of Phantos.) Finkel went on to indict the Pajama Gang for a long list of crimes. He condemned their fakery. He bewailed their graffiti. He denounced their ideas as dangerous to the impressionable youth of the Unum.

The irony of professing to care about children while at the same time demonizing a group of harmless orphans was, of course, lost upon the sleepwalkers. They rejoiced at the news. They celebrated. One man, whom we know as Uncle Norman, grabbed his wife, whom we know as Aunt Millie, and kissed her passionately—something he had never done, at least in the dreamworld.

And the impressionable youth of the Unum proved themselves, indeed, impressionable. Goaded by their president into hatred, they jumped up and down like wild baboons and begged their parents to take them outside to see the Pajama Gangsters jailed. "Please, Dad, pretty please, Mom!" they begged. "Can't we go and see those rotten kids thrown in the slammer?" Well, the parents could hardly say no. It was the height of good parenting to set before your child's eyes an example of a bad apple, and the Pajama Gang was an orchard.

Now you may be wondering if the President Finkel on the news was Harold Dore or Phantos. In truth, whether it was Harold in disguise or Phantos in disguise hardly mattered. Finkel was a costume, a rubbery Halloween mask that either one of them could put on. But to answer your question, today Phantos was wearing the mask. Phantos, as you recall, mistrusted Harold's sympathies for humanity and so sidelined him for the day. Where, or rather who, was Harold then, on this Sunday morning? We shall see shortly.

Even before the prisoners appeared, the sidewalks were flooded. All of New Shiny City was outside, which never happened. The people cheered and waved Unum flags and sang the Unum anthem and bumped fists in solidarity. The youths, wearing their black school uniforms, if only to appear upright compared to the slovenly Pajama Gangsters, stockpiled trash from the gutters to hurl at the criminals. Ohers waved posters with taunting messages, such as, "Losers wear bathrobes!" and "You're going to jail!" and, probably the most offensive, "This is Reality: Wake up!"

This circus was not just a local affair. It was televised. All over the Unum, no matter the time zone, people were glued to their screens, watching "breaking news" of the Pajama Gang's long walk of shame.

The walk began at the 99th Precinct, where the Pajama Gang had been detained following the raid at Mount Nightlight. Amidst a flurry of Red Suits, reporters, and rubberneckers, the prisoners exited the building. They exited in twos, and the first two were Orion and Hermit. Phantos wanted the Pajama Gang to be seen in their native dress, so Orion still wore his striped pajamas and Hermit still had on his baby-blue ones. The only items the children lacked for were their flight pillows and bags of sand, for these had been deemed "illegal weapons" and confiscated by Safety Enforcement.

The tall boy and the short boy toddled forward, for it was difficult to walk with leg irons. Orion and Hermit were shackled together at the ankles, and their chains extended down the line of Lucids, forming an impressive chain gang of 316 youths.

When they were all outside and arrayed on the avenue, Commissioner Sikman climbed out of a squad car and came forward to meet them. With his leather jacket and starred cap and batlike ears and charcoal eyes, he bade the children to march and march well. The whole world was watching them, he warned, and they could expect no mercy if they tried to run away. Of course, like everything mares said, this was a blatant lie. They could expect no mercy, no matter what they did.

Glum and unhappy and stumbling in their ankle chains, the Lucids lumbered down the avenue. Commissioner Sikman marched in front of them, flanked by four sergeants and as many squad cars. The rest of the police cars—and there were many—followed behind the Lucids and honked their horns whenever the children's pace slackened.

Oh, if Remmy could have seen his lightbearers now! He would have wept in sorrow! He would have howled in indignation! To see his bright pupils being paraded before the masses, being jeered and vilified by the same people whom they were trying to save, might well have changed the Dream Guardian's opinion of the human race for good. Fortunately, he was not there, and his opinion of us remained a favorable one.

As the Pajama Gang slogged north toward the capital, their chains clinking and clanking, the crowds they encountered were not content to harass them and let them go. No, they wished to pursue them. They wished to heckle them in ever increasing droves all the way to Finkel Mansion. And, so, they did. At one point, when the "Pajama Chain Gang," as they were now mockingly called, were crossing the chessboard squares of the Board, Hermit glanced over his shoulder and beheld an angry sea, frothing and spraying and hissing! Then he blinked his eyes and saw the mob, which was scarier.

At last, the exodus was over. After 11 miles, 39 yards, 2 feet, and 5 inches, after 324 projectiles, 456 threats, 105,570 jeers, and 200,999 scowls, the prisoners arrived at the gates of Finkel Mansion. If not for the training they had received at Mount Nightlight—which taught them never to take the dreamworld too seriously, for it was, after all, only an illusion—surely, they would have fallen apart by now. But Lucids were strong and perceptive, four-foot warriors of the soul! Although they looked spent and some a bit teary, their chins were up, every one of them.

He was there waiting for them, President Finkel. Or, rather, Phantos in the Finkel costume. He stood at a podium, elevated on a high platform, which could only be accessed via a ramp. Bodyguards in sunglasses stood stiffly at his sides, while, behind him, on the mansion lawn, a brigade of soldiers displayed rifles, machineguns, grenade launchers, and other shows of force.

Commissioner Sikman nodded to the President, then gestured to the Lucids. The youths were still arrayed in two columns, still chained, still in their pajamas. And all around the youths, hemming them in, pressing closer and closer and shouting rabidly at them were the people. And in every home and building in the Unum, the people were likewise shouting at their screens.

President Finkel raised his hand, and just as if he had pressed a Mute button, the crowd hushed.

"Thank you," he said, adjusting the podium's microphone. There were numerous speakers stationed throughout the city, such that all heard Finkel loudly and clearly, whether they wanted to or not. "My safe and loyal citizens, today is a rare and special day. A day of justice. A day of reckoning. A day of triumph!"

He lowered his hand, at which the crowd unmuted itself and roared like a zoo at feeding time.

"Now, then," said Finkel, "on to the trial."

Nine magistrates, in somber robes and funny white wigs, trotted up to the podium. It would be tedious and extremely boring to repeat their words, for each magistrate had a chance to speak and each was longwinded and tone-deaf and as charismatic as a skeleton in a museum. Moreover, I'm sure you could predict, as could every last person assembled there, Lucids included, that they would pronounce the accused guilty. Therefore, we'll skip it.

"10,000 years to life!" declared the ninth and final magistrate.

It was a preposterous sentence; the average life expectancy in the Unum was only fifty-six years. Nonetheless, the unthinking people applauded it.

When the magistrates retired, President Finkel retook the podium and asked the Lucids whether they had anything to say for themselves before they were locked up for ten millennia. He smiled diabolically at them, awaiting their answer. The demon, you see, wanted to break them. Something about the Lucids' chins and the upward angle at which they were held irritated her. This was the moment when these punks were supposed to weep, to confess their wrongdoings and beg for mercy. It is not that Phantos despised their strength or envied it; rather, it was that, for all her immense power, she feared it.

"Nothing to say for yourselves?" he shouted. "No apology? No remorse? Speak, you terrorists! Speak, you anarchists! Speak, you traitors! Speak, you lying, fear-mongering, pot-stirring, pillow-hugging savages! Speak!!!"

We cannot rightly say whether one or two of Remmy's pupils would have, with a little more time, crumbled under Finkel's browbeating. Maybe they would have, maybe they wouldn't. In any event, the President's diatribe was cut short. For Suzy and Sky had arrived.

"There's more!" someone shouted.

"Two more!" cried another.

"Two more criminals!" shouted a third.

Suzy and Sky advanced through the mob. They suffered as much ridicule as their fellow Lucids had during their march from the precinct. They were shoved and mocked and berated as they approached the podium. Nonetheless, they remained undaunted. Although the girls' pajamas were of the softest materials, their souls were girded in steel.

Hermit and Orion, when they saw Suzy and Sky, were flabbergasted. Their peers were equally dumbstruck. Why had these two come here, to be imprisoned and to have their imprisonment livestreamed to the world? They were free; they had escaped capture; and, now, they were subjecting themselves to chains?

Finkel—that is, Phantos—recognized Sky and Suzy at a glance. Sky was the girl she had beguiled into disclosing the location of Mount Nightlight; Suzy was the girl she had stuck inside a doubledream. She was aware of Suzy's escape, and, though baffling, it did not greatly inconvenience the demon. After all, Phantos had caught Remulus, and was not a Dream Guardian a greater prize than a mere human?

President Finkel quipped into his microphone: "Well, look what we have here! A couple of stragglers to join the slumber party!"

The crowd yucked it up. Their laughter made Suzy's ears ring. She glanced leerily at Sky and Sky glanced leerily at her. In this moment, neither was very confident that their plan would work, especially as the jets were nowhere in sight.

What delayed them? Had Harold changed his mind and canceled his request for planes? Or had he double-crossed them and never issued the command to begin with? Was that all this was? An elaborate set-up to facilitate their surrender?

President Finkel sought to make an example of his new captives and, therefore, ordered that a microphone be given to Suzy and Sky. Then, in a fiery tone, he demanded the girls answer for their crimes.

"We have nothing to say to you," Suzy told Finkel, speaking into the wireless mic. "But to the people, we wish to say this: Look around you. What do you see? I see guns and I see tyranny. I see gray skies and gray streets. I see people who've lost the ability to think with their hearts. I see so much fear and so little love. This isn't my dream. Is it yours?" she asked Sky.

Sky shook her braids side to side.

"Is it yours?" Suzy asked the Lucids, and resoundingly they cried, "NO!"

Suzy resumed: "It's not our dream, and it isn't yours either. It's *his* dream," and she pointed at Finkel, "and it is a nightmare. But we have the power to wake up. That power is ours. And when we wake up, I promise you, it will be to a brand-new world, where people are free and unafraid!"

"Where people are strong and wise!" Sky chimed in.

"And where," said Suzy, "the sky is blue and the grass so clean you can eat off it!"

"Amen!" cried Sky, sharing the mic.

"You are a gazillion times more than you think you are!" Suzy told the crowd. "You are amazing beings! Your potential is unlimited!"

The Lucids were nearly in tears hearing Suzy and Sky's speech, which echoed the teachings of their favorite blue lynx. The sleepwalkers, on the other hand, deemed it nonsense. They clucked their tongues and shook their heads. A certain pigtailed woman and balding man, crushed in the thick of the crowd, covered their faces in shame, lest they be identified as the aunt and uncle of one of the girls.

Phantos, wholly unexpecting such a spirited reply, was nevertheless a clever demon and, as President Finkel, made this rebuttal:

"Felons," he wailed, "you parrot the worst sort of conspiracy theories! But if this is, as you claim, a dream, then prove it! You gangsters believe you can fly, is that right? I believe a demonstration is in order."

Suzy took the bait. She untied the pillow from her back. She took off running, she squeezed her pillow and dove onto it, with every expectation of ascending like a bird. But for some strange reason, the wings did not manifest, and Suzy flopped onto the concrete.

Everyone watching, both in the streets and in their homes, fell into fits of laughter.

"No matter," said Finkel, snickering, "perhaps, there is still another trick up your robe sleeve. Your graffiti, for example. You believe it is magic, eh? Why not show the people how magical it is?"

This time Sky took the bait. She dug into the pocket of her kimono and whipped out a can of Dreamffiti. Crouching, she shook the can and prepared to paint the pavement. But the second she pressed the valve, the can exploded and spat a rainbow of paint in every direction. Sky's face was splattered.

"No matter!" cried Finkel, over the deliriously laughing crowd. "There is still one more hope, I think, for your case. I have heard it said that you gangsters treasure, above all, sand. Dreamsand, as you style it. Please, for the edification of myself and the whole world that is watching, show us the magic of your sand!"

By now, Suzy and Sky grasped what was happening: somehow, the demon was interfering with their dream totems. Phantos was making them look crazy and foolish, and, thus, driving a wedge between them and the people.

Again, Suzy and Sky checked the airspace over the capital.

Still, not a single jet in sight.

"They get lost or something?" Sky whispered.

"I don't know," Suzy returned.

"Can't believe we trusted Harold Dore," grumbled Sky. "What were we thinking!"

"Will you," persisted Finkel, "or will you not show us the magic of your dreamsand? If not, we must infer that you are, indeed, liars and charlatans."

Suzy saw plainly she had no choice but to try.

For the sleepwalkers, it was a bizarre and pathetic spectacle to watch the short blonde girl in the red bathrobe dump sand on herself. Nothing happened, of course, thanks to Phantos. Suzy did not grow any larger than she already was. In fact, being so humiliated, she might have lost an inch.

"Police Commissioner," the President said to Sikman, "arrest these two criminals. Shackle them with the others and get them gone! To jail, I say! Jail!"

The sleepwalkers parroted him. "Jail!" they screamed. "Jail! Jail!"

While Sikman and the Red Suits were carrying out this order and prodding Suzy and Sky toward the disgraced youths, Hermit, who had watched the entire fiasco with his breath bottled up in his chest like a fizzy soda, sneezed.

Something had fallen onto his nose and tickled it.

He looked up. And there, in the gray dome of the sky, was a jet plane.

Chapter Eighteen

Uprising

No sooner had Hermit observed the jet than he perceived a second. And a third. And a fourth. Swiveling his head, he spotted several more military planes approaching from the south. Were the skyscrapers not blocking his view, he would have seen ten more.

As the jets crossed the sky, they left behind long trails of snowlike powder. Hermit, at first, assumed this was the usual stuff—more pollution. Orion, staring in the same direction as Hermit, thought differently. He opined that the powder was way too sparkly and pretty to be Finkel's nasty pollutants. "Gotta be soul sand," Orion concluded.

Hermit nodded enthusiastically—it *was* soul sand. He turned and reported this intelligence to the pair shackled behind them, who in turn reported it to the Lucids behind them, and so on down the line.

The sand sifted down through the sky. With a soft pelting sound, quieter than rain, it settled onto rooftops and rain gutters, onto windshields and traffic lights, and onto the streets. And as everyone in the city was, on this festive day, in the streets, it settled also upon them.

It was a subtle precipitation. Many did not notice it, while those that did dismissed it as just another variety of toxic fallout—nothing to lose sleep over. The sand collected on their hats and on their heads. It stuck like dandruff to the wigs of the magistrates and marred the immaculate suit of President Finkel.

More subtle still, the sand found its way into mouths and noses and lungs. It caused salvos of sneezes and a curious grainy texture on many a tongue. One scientific toddler even drew his forefinger through the stuff, as it lay scattered on the ground, and tasted it. Had anyone gazed at the boy's face and witnessed the blissful smile blooming there, they might have guessed what they were in for.

And how did the Lucids react to this totally unexpected manifestation of the most marvelous, most mystical, most beautiful sand of all?

With joy, of course! They beamed at one another. They tilted back their heads so that the sand would fall upon their foreheads, their third eyes, the exact spot where, during their initiations, Remmy had rubbed sand upon them and whisked them away on glorious journeys of the soul.

Suzy and Sky were enormously relieved. Harold Dore had not forgotten them, after all. As soon as the Red Suits marched them to the front of the chain gang and clapped their shackles on, they hugged Orion and Hermit, who were directly behind them. Then a brief conference among the four ensued. Suzy explained to the boys how and why it had come to pass that the Unum Air Force was spraying soul sand. When Orion had heard it all, he paid Suzy the highest compliment he had ever given her, saying, "Not bad for a Sleeping Beauty!"

Such jollity among these kids, such exuberance and good cheer…it was inexplicable to the crowd and to those watching at home. Were these kids positively insane? They were in leg irons, about to be jailed for the rest of their lives, and here they were all hugs and smiles!

President Finkel sensed what was happening and scowled viciously. The sand, as it touched his neck and face and knuckles, burned the creature inside. What was good and healing for the human was noxious to Phantos. Soul sand might never kill such a powerful demon, no; but it could and did torture her.

"*Harold*," snarled Finkel, glaring at the planes with an itch to blow them up at a flick of his finger. "This is his doing!" Vowing to deal with that man later, Finkel returned his attention to the Pajama Gang. They were celebrating! They were laughing! They were giving hugs and high-fives! This looked bad. Very bad. And what, Finkel wondered, might the soul sand do to the people gathered in the streets? He had to send them home. He had to cut the livestream. He had to get those pajama kids out of here, ASAP!

"Sikman!" he hollered from the podium, "remove those pillow-huggers—NOW!"

Sikman and his Red Suits complied, and with predictable brutishness. Threatening with their batons and stun guns, they herded the Lucids toward a fleet of police vans. Ah, but the youths they accosted now were not the same as they were before. They were fired up, jazzed up, juiced up, high on soul sand and the beauty and wonder and interconnectedness of the universe! Thus, they resisted. Thus, they dragged their heels. Thus, they implored the Red Suits to follow their own consciences and not obey an authority when that authority is unjust.

In short, they created quite the hullabaloo. Imagine, now, imagine over 300 youths in pajamas, chained together like animals, struggling body and soul with armored police in riot gear, all the while a shimmering white sand was falling from the sky like diamonds.

Then, my friends, it happened.

It finally, finally happened.

Someone in the crowd—an anonymous hero, whose identity, gender, age, and occupation shall never be recorded in history books, but who could well have been you or me—one person, I say, broke the spell and shouted, almost without thinking, like a reflex, like one starting up in bed with a sudden jolt of truth, *"Hey! They're just kids!"*

A match thrown onto several trillion metric tons of newspaper—such was the effect of this one fiery voice upon the crowd.

It was almost as if a light switch had been turned on, and everyone could see again. And what they saw was an abomination.

"Stop that!" cried an old man. "They've done nothing wrong!"

"Careful!" screamed a young woman. "Quit pushing them, you could hurt them!"

"I'm recording this!" warned a teenager, pointing his cell phone.

More and more people rushed to the defense of the Pajama Gang. At first, there were only a handful of protestors, sprinkled throughout the multitudes. But as each new person spoke out, a curious thing happened: his or her neighbors grew emboldened and added their voices to the others.

"Don't hurt them!" cried a young man, who earlier had whipped a stone at Orion.

"Where's your humanity?" a journalist bellowed, who had previously heckled the Pajama Gang for hours.

"Justice for the Pajama Gang!" screeched a mother, who had only a few minutes ago cheered their incarceration.

Then a certain pigtailed woman, whom we know as Aunt Millie, and a certain balding man, whom we know as Uncle Norman, loudly proclaimed that they were the nearest and dearest kin of one of the Pajama Gang members. "We have to protect our niece!" they shouted to the crowd. "Please help us!" And together, with their son Braydon and a militia of hundreds, growing to thousands, they stormed the mansion gates, demanding, "FREE THE CHILDREN! FREE THE CHILDREN! FREE THE CHILDREN!"

The people watching around the world, on their TVs and computers and phones and smart-glasses and watches, were agog. They had not been misted with soul sand, of course, and therefore, frowned upon the protest. It was unheard of to question, to challenge, to demand. And yet…there was something stirring about the protest, something inspiring that touched their slumbering humanity. They wanted to turn off the news, but they couldn't. They felt obliged to condemn the protestors, but they didn't. They knew they should wad their ears with cotton balls, but the voice of the people was too powerful, too soulful, too beautiful to ignore.

"FREE THE CHILDREN! FREE THE CHILDREN! FREE THE CHILDREN!"

Shouting this phrase, the protestors pressed toward the Red Suits. Whether it was from fear of the multitude or whether the sand had somehow penetrated their armor and reached their hearts, the Red Suits stood down. They lowered their weapons and backed away from the Pajama Gang.

But it was Sikman who held the keys to the Lucids' shackles. The crowd demanded that the Police Commissioner hand them over, not knowing that he was a mare and would be more likely to eat the children than to free them. Unholstering his pistol, Sikman waved it at the protestors and cried, "Back! Get back! Or I'll blow you back with bullets!"

Sikman's chamber, however, held only 18 rounds, and there were at least a hundred times that number confronting him. The people surged toward him. He pulled the trigger. His barrel flashed. The bullet went astray. The people wrested from him the pistol and the keys too, then rained blows upon the villain and threw him aside like yesterday's trash.

The protestors were winning.

President Finkel, who had been turning darker and darker shades of red this whole time, called upon his generals. "Fire upon them! Fire on those agitators! Disperse them all!"

On the mansion lawn the generals signaled to the infantry. Reluctantly, the soldiers raised their rifles and machineguns and grenade launchers. They did not wish to fire on the innocent, yet they were trained to follow orders and that was what they intended to do. It was fortunate, then, for the sake of both the Lucids and the protestors that, at this point in the story, a tall, broad-shouldered man pushed to the front of the crowd. He had on a gray suit and red necktie and his face was obscured by the ballcap he wore.

The soldiers adjusted their aims ever so slightly. The brazen man in the suit would be their first target, their bullseye.

But then this man removed his cap and lifted his head and revealed to the soldiers the face of their Commander in Chief.

President Art Q. Finkel.

A second President Art Q. Finkel.

Suzy's jaw fell. Sky's jaw fell. Orion's and Hermit's jaws fell.

The original Finkel's jaw fell too.

The crowd staggered back, gasping. The soldiers slowly lowered their weapons. They glanced back and forth, several times, between the first Finkel standing with his bodyguards and the second Finkel standing with the Pajama Gang.

"Imposter!" shrieked the first Finkel, visibly panicking. "Impersonator! Charlatan! Pay him no mind!"

The second Finkel turned to the crowd. "President Finkel," he cried, "is a fiction! There is no Finkel, see!" At this, he shapeshifted from a large and handsome man in a business suit to a pale and lank man in a black T-shirt whose text read, "I'D RATHER BE SLEEPING."

"Harold!" cried Suzy.

The young man smiled at Suzy. "What? You think I'd miss this?"

The crowd was stunned but not incredulous. Having felt and drank and breathed the soul sand, they had become wise and perceptive. As such, they took this doubling of their president as confirmation that this was, as the little blonde girl had insisted, just a dream. Many imparted to their neighbors or thought aloud, "We *must* be dreaming!"

"But if there is no Finkel," cried Uncle Norman, who had worshiped the man along with everyone else in the Unum, "then who the heck is that?" And he jerked his thumb at the first Finkel.

Phantos—realizing that one of her grandest illusions, that of an all-powerful leader laboring for the good of the people, was shattered; realizing, too, that on this day all things would be revealed—took off her rubber mask. She transformed into that sly pixie girl in the black jumpsuit and jester cap, whose face was as white as the dead and whose smile was as dark as the devil's.

Twirling her magician's wand, Phantos shot up into the air and cackled like a witch. The cackle was supernatural. It came not from her black lips but from the sky. It was heard not merely in New Shiny City, but in every city and in every home on the planet.

At the same time, a fierce gale whipped through the capital, which became a sort of dust storm owing to all the sand. People shielded their eyes. Women held down their skirts. Men held down their hats and toupees. Trash poured like rapids through the streets. Storm clouds blotted the sun. Thunder and lightning burst from above, and all was as dark as night.

"Who am I?" shrieked Phantos, responding to Uncle Norman's question. "I am PHANTOS, Lord of Illusion and Ruler of the Undreamt! I am your Master, and you shall know my wrath!"

Then Phantos, with her long black fingernails, carved a hole in the air beside her—a black hole, much like the kind Harold cut with his magic scissors. And from this hole flew wicked beasts, beasts of various descriptions, yet all hairy and winged, red-eyed and fanged! They were mares, and they were at least double the size of an average human. They flew circles about the people, intimidating them with growls and hisses and now and then snatching some unfortunate aloft into the air.

Meanwhile, the mares already present outside Finkel Mansion—principally, the generals, the magistrates, and a handful of other top brass—shed their human disguises. Beating their leathery wings, they joined their evil brethren in the sky.

There is still one illusion left, thought Phantos, as she watched with wicked delight her minions terrorize the people.

The ultimate illusion!

The mother of all fear!

With a piercing laugh, which was heard by every human being in the Unum, Phantos dove at the podium and blasted through the wooden stage and dropped out of sight.

"Did she go away?" asked Suzy, wishing with all her heart it were so.

"Don't bet your pillow," replied Harold.

Just then, the ground near the stage quaked. The children, still in chains, shuffled backwards as fast as their feet could move.

Suddenly, the concrete cracked and heaved apart and from the bowels of the earth unfolded a gigantic beast, which paralyzed all with the utmost fear.

It was not simply that it was as tall as the tallest building in the Unum or that its skin was scaly red or that its jaws were multiple, each nested inside the other like a Russian doll, or that its teeth, covered in barnacles and the carcasses of whales, could bite through metal.

The terror it inspired reached deeper. For as long as anyone could remember, they were taught to fear the sea monster that haunted the shores of their great nation.

And here, seemingly reborn, and fitted for land with a hundred centipede-like legs, was the creature called Nemesis.

CHAPTER NINETEEN

THE ULTIMATE ILLUSION, AND HOW TO OVERCOME IT

A shockwave of horror went through the people. Nothing could have terrified them more than the reappearance of this monstrous boogeyman. Suzy, with a backward glance, observed the overwhelming effect Nemesis had on them. In a matter of seconds, their love and strength and unity, which had been so inspiring to see, had deformed into selfish survivalism, with each person shoving his or her neighbor in the back and screaming, "Get out of the way, you moron! Move it! Run!"

But, of course, no one *could* run. They were packed into the square like pickles in a jar. With such congestion, no one could gain an inch. Consequently, they became abusive with one another, throwing elbows and assigning blame. They also became rather stupid. Many called out, "Finkel, save us!" never mind that Finkel did not exist. Most discouraging of all, no one seemed to remember the wisdom of the little blonde girl, who had revealed that this world was but a passing dream.

"If this keeps up," Suzy thought, with mounting distress, "all that we've achieved will be undone!"

Suzy looked down the row of Lucids, looked into the faces of the boys and girls who were her brothers and sisters and cried, "Be the example for the others! Stand your ground! And never forget what Remmy taught us!"

They were still chained together, and, as one unit, they stood together, all in a row, directly before Nemesis and its many slobbering mouths.

Then Suzy shut her eyes. She shut her eyes as she had before, during life-and-death moments, whether it was hiding from Commissioner Sikman in the janitor's closet or plunging down the mountainside during her first attempt at flight. She closed her eyes and loudly, so her friends could hear, spoke these words:

"It's just a dream, and we're not afraid."

She said them again.

"It's just a dream, and we're not afraid."

And she said them again.

Sky lent her voice to Suzy's. Orion and Hermit did too. Pretty soon all 318 Lucids had their eyes closed and lips moving to these special words.

"IT'S JUST A DREAM, AND WE'RE NOT AFRAID."

When those in the crowd nearest the Lucids heard their chant, and when they saw them standing together hand in hand, in spite of the monster that drooled over them, they were astonished. It occurred to them that if they were destined to be devoured, it would be infinitely better to spend their last few minutes doing as these children were doing and showing love and courage and strength.

And, so, they did.

Harold joined hands with Uncle Norman and Uncle Norman with Aunt Millie and Aunt Millie with Braydon and Braydon with a Red Suit, who removed his face shield so the boy could see that he was, after all, only human.

Neighbor and neighbor quit their bickering and fighting and linked hands. Then, closing their eyes, they uttered the special words.

"IT'S JUST A DREAM, AND WE'RE NOT AFRAID."

The Lucids had set an example for the people nearest them in the crowd, who then inspired those farther back to do the same. Soon everyone in New Shiny City was holdings hands and saying these affirmative words. And, as the cameras had never stopped rolling, everyone watching at home was doing the same.

"IT'S JUST A DREAM, AND WE'RE NOT AFRAID."

Make no mistake, the words were not simply affirmative; they were a kind of protective spell. For when Phantos, now in the costume of Nemesis, realized that the terror she wrought was weakening before a more powerful force, that of brotherly love, she roared a terrible roar and pounced at the Lucids and meant to swallow them up, bath slippers and all!

I would ask you now to freeze-frame this scene. A thousand-ton monster has just launched itself into the air, directly over a crowd of innocent youths and reformed grownups, and not a one cared.

No one saw the monster, for their eyes were closed. For all intents and purposes, the monster did not exist. Death was right in front of them, and they did not give a flying pillow. An illusion only works if we give it our attention, and these fine folks gave it zilch. The hour of awakening was at hand.

Let us unfreeze the scene and direct our attention skyward, where a beam, originating from a rift in the heavens, shot through the darkness and struck Nemesis in mid-leap. She howled such that all the glass windows in the city shattered at once and, reeling backwards, landed atop Finkel Mansion, flattening that stately building to the ground.

Nemesis flailed on her back like an overturned beetle. With her sole and only eye, she squinted up at the light shining from above.

It was an awful light, a wicked and blinding light, if you happened to be the Lord of Illusion. Otherwise, it was simply glorious.

Not that any human saw it. They were still chanting with their eyes closed. But the curious thing was that the longer they chanted, the more intense the light became. The sky stretched apart and the rift became a gulf, while the light that poured out of it shone ever wider and ever brighter.

The mares, flapping fiendishly in the air, tried to evade the light. They ducked, they swooped, they dodged and maneuvered—all to no avail. For when the light broadened to cover the entirety of the square, they were caught in it. Where the light touched them, smoke arose. It burned them, and they dropped hissing from the sky like bugs acquainted with an electric zapper. Where they hit the ground, they began to deteriorate and dissolve. They paled and paled. They became gray like cinder flakes, then gusted away into nothingness, which, of course, was what they were at bottom.

In like fashion, Phantos withered under the light. For while light encourages the growth of good things, like plants and animals, light disinfects and kills that which is evil. The light was eroding her, as it had her minions. It scalded her carapace. It seared her spiny tail and burned her hundredfold legs. She was shrinking, melting, diminishing before the heavenly light. And it was all that wicked little girl's fault! If Phantos could just mount one last attack, if she could just smite that one little girl, the chief rebel, the rest would crumble. She flipped upright and thundered toward Suzy, angrier than ever.

Still, she was not the same monster as before…each step was an agony and a trial. As she stalked toward the girl in the red bathrobe, Phantos felt herself growing smaller and smaller. Smoke rolled off her. Her whole chitinous body was puffing like a power plant. Once the awesome height of a skyscraper, she was now no taller than a giraffe—a very average giraffe. This size being further reduced to that of a very average bear, Phantos reacted in desperation. She reared up, as best she could on her disintegrating hindlegs, and screeched:

"Look at me! Open your eyes— look!—and be afraid! Oh, you wretched humans! Oh, you unquestioning sleepers! On that cold, thoughtless day when truth becomes lie, on that day of infamous ignorance, when none shall question and all shall obey, we will meet again!!!"

So saying, the demon—shorter than even Suzy at this point—revealed to the people, whose eyes were closed and who were paying her no mind, nor attending to her speech, what was perhaps her real form: *a shadow*.

Then, with an insane peal of laughter and pain, Phantos went the way of dust.

CHAPTER TWENTY

SLEEPERS, AWAKE!

Although we may cheer the demon's defeat, and rightly so, there was no celebration among Suzy and her friends, nor among the people. Not yet anyway. They were all still clasping hands and chanting, and probably would have continued doing so for a whole day and night, were it not for the extraordinary wake-up call they received.

It was not really a wake-up call in the singular sense. There were many wake-up calls, all heard at once.

It began, powerfully, with church chimes.

Then came twittering songbirds and mooing cows and the crowing of roosters.

To this were joined the ring-ring-ring of alarm bells, the tap-tap-tap of sticks on windows, and the beep-beep-beep of digital clocks. There were boisterous radio disc-jockeys and staticky music and the repetitive cry of "Cuckoo! Cuckoo!" There was a mother—whose I don't know—crying, "Time to wake up!" And there was an unknown father too, saying the same, though in a sterner voice. There were the whisper of wind and the burble of water and the buzzing of winged creatures. And through it all a chorus of children laughing.

These were the merry sounds of morning. Since the dawn of time, they have told humanity, one way or another, to wake up. And, so, they told them now.

Everyone opened their eyes.

Everyone looked up.

The heavens beckoned to them with its golden light and celestial vortex. It didn't take a genius to understand that, whatever lay on the other side of that portal, it was a freer, greener, and truer place than the Unum.

The Lucids glowed at one another, with smiles so big they hurt their cheekbones. No one said, "Ah-ha! There's the Liminal Place!" just as no one ever says, "Ah-ha! There's the sky!" or "Ah-ha! There's the ground!" It was that obvious.

Then Hermit, brushing aside his shaggy hair so he could see, cried out, "Look!"

He motioned to the black hole, the portal to the Undreamt that Phantos had carved with her nails. Fluttering out of the hole came heaps and droves of tiny luminous beings. The Nyxies, for such they were, sang in jubilation:

> *Rejoice! Rejoice! Morning's here!*
> *Hug a friend and give a cheer,*
> *Rouse yourselves, for goodness' sake,*
> *Sleepers! Sleepers! Time to wake!*

The people were mesmerized. All marveled at the Nyxies as they trilled musically about them and pulsed with light.

"The Nyxies!" cried Suzy, clapping her hands together, for she had dreaded that they had been slain during the siege of Mount Nightlight. "They're alive! Oh, and listen to them sing! So beautifully!"

And it was precisely because of this compliment that Ulala flew straight to Suzy and alighted on her outstretched palm. She decided Suzy was her favorite this time and dropped a curtsy to the girl.

Though the Nyxies' reappearance was, indeed, comforting to the Lucids, it would be a lie to say they weren't thinking of their teacher.

"But where's Remmy?" Sky inquired of Ulala. "Didn't he make it? He had to!"

The Lucids, every one of them, grew quiet. Their looks became heavy, though none as heavy as Sky's. All attended to the Nyxie's response, which she gave with a little knowing smirk and a backward glance at the hole.

Then the Lucids witnessed awesome beings soar from the black hole—huge beings of golden light, each sporting several wings and several arms and having, vaguely, a human shape. These magnificent characters, which were translucent like spirits and almost defied description, dispersed amongst the crowd and began shepherding them to where they must be going. They rose upward and the humans, holding fast to their many wings and many arms, rose with them. They floated toward the Liminal Place and the great unknown that awaited them. The people were not afraid, though. All were as children. All were reborn. All were forgiven.

As the Lucids easily deduced, these beings were the Dream Guardians—the ones Phantos had imprisoned in the Undreamt.

The last of the Guardians to exit the hole swooped to the spot where the Lucids were gathered. As it alighted, there was a blinding flash of light, which, when it dimmed, revealed a familiar blue lynx in a familiar orange robe.

"Why these low faces?" growled Remmy, staring round at his pupils. "And why these chains! Away, I say, away with all things heavy!"

And throwing out his paws, Remmy made it so. The children's chains shattered, and their frowns lifted. Freed at last, they rushed forth and tackled Remmy. They waylaid him with hugs and kisses and chin-scratches, and all was as light and joyous as Remmy had wished them to be—except one.

Sky stood apart, staring morosely at her slippers. Remmy, begging the children to clear some space, approached her. He stooped over her and imparted something in her ear. Sky was seen to gasp, then to smile, then to cry elatedly. Suzy, watching, wondered what he had told her. Remmy then looked around at the youths and said in a tone that was bittersweet, "Lightbearers, my children, it is time we must part."

They nodded in understanding. Though none wished to say goodbye to Remulus, they were at the same time anxious to join the others in the place they had long sought and affectionately called Wakesville.

The Lucids shared a look of hesitation with each other, wondering who would be adventurous enough to go first.

"Slowpokes!" teased Orion, as his feet left the ground. "Last one to Wakesville is a dumb drifter! And look, Remmy, no pillow! Ain't that prime!"

This spurred the others just fine. Giggling, they bounded into the air, racing after the sandy-haired rascal in the striped pajamas. Hermit hugged Suzy and Sky, each in turn, then peered uncertainly at the kaleidoscope of colorful lights above him. As if he were already half gone, he remarked, "I wonder what Mama made for dinner." Then, like a helium balloon, he left.

At this point, Suzy expected to say farewell to Sky. But when she pivoted to the girl, all she saw were Sky's purple slippers.

"Sorry!" Sky apologized as she ascended into the air. "I'm just no good at goodbyes! It's been real, hasn't it?"

Suzy was about to correct her and say that, no, it had been far from *real*, however Sky got in the last word, crying out, as she neared the Liminal Place, "Love ya, Snoozy!"

When Suzy looked away from her dear friends, with damp eyes, she was surprised to find Harold Dore standing next to her. Harold regarded Remmy and Remmy regarded Harold, quietly, tensely, neither saying a word. Then Remmy, breaking the silence, said, "Nice shirt."

You will recall that Harold wore a black T-shirt with the tagline, "I'D RATHER BE SLEEPING."

"Thanks," said Harold. "But, no offense, the first thing I'm gonna do when I get back is throw it out."

"Good idea," commented Suzy.

"I second that," said Remmy.

"I owe you everything," Harold told Suzy. "You and your Pajama Gang."

Remmy cleared his throat in a loud manner. It was practically a growl.

"Lucids, I mean," Harold interjected, which seemed to satisfy the lynx.

"We couldn't have done it without you," Suzy told him. "And, no offence, but I hope you never become President of Wakesville, if there is such a thing."

The odd, lonely daydreamer who was Harold Dore chuckled over this and said, "You can bet your pillow." He then directed his attention to the Liminal Place and murmured, "Well, here goes." And, with that, he was gone.

"That was mighty clever of you," Remmy told Suzy, when they were at last alone—quite possibly the only two left in the Unum. He bent over and rubbed his paw in the sand that dusted the ground like snow. "I never would have thought of it, not in a million dreams!"

Suzy, receiving such high praise from her mentor, blushed and lowered her head ever so slightly.

"Remmy? Can I ask you a question, just one last question, for old time's sake?"

Remmy grinned, displaying his four canines. "Why, of course."

She gazed earnestly into his golden eyes. "When I wake, will I remember any of this?"

"None of you shall," replied Remmy. "And so much the better, or else how could you get on in that pleasant life ahead, thinking of all the crazy, cockamamie stuff that happened here? The Red Suits, the mares, Nemesis, and Phantos...Yes, some dreams are best forgotten."

"But not you," came Suzy's choked reply. "I don't want to forget you."

Remmy's paw was still powdered with soul sand when he touched it to Suzy's forehead and intoned, in a voice that crackled and warmed like fire, "The lessons you learned—the truths—that is what you must and shall remember, always."

She threw her arms around him, whereupon Remmy scooped her up and embraced her. She pressed her cheek against his silken bathrobe and inhaled his sandalwood smell, wanting desperately to hold onto the way he smelled and the way he felt and the way he spoke. She loved him so much, though she could hardly say what he really was. Maybe he was, in the end, only the way to the truth. And this, as he himself had told her, she would never forget.

"Someday," he whispered in her ear, "we will meet again. And I will tell you and the others unbelievable tales, tales of courage, friendship, and heroic deeds."

"But where will we meet?" Suzy wondered aloud.

"Why," said the lynx, winking at her, "in the only place we can!"

Hearing this, Suzy gathered why Sky had looked so happy after speaking with Remmy. Doubtless, he had told her the same. The promise that they would all reunite on some red-letter night in the dreamworld made their parting that much easier for Suzy and, certainly, for Remmy too.

Remmy glanced up at the Liminal Place, at the river of souls passing through the tunnel of golden light. "It is getting late, Suzy. The souls in deep sleep are waking, and you wouldn't want to keep your mom and dad waiting."

At the mention of her parents, Suzy was taken aback. What with all the terrors and tears of the day, which was the wild conclusion to her wild adventure, Suzy had forgotten why she had undertaken the adventure in the first place. Her parents! She would be with them soon, so very soon! She could hardly contain her excitement. She felt as light as air—lighter actually, which is why she promptly slipped through Remmy's paws and floated upward. She lifted higher and higher, while Remmy became smaller and smaller, until he was but a blue dot on a white square.

Waving down to Remmy, Suzy noticed something incredible: her poor left foot, which had to make do with several layers of socks for the entirety of this story and, consequently, to suffer sores and chills and blisters, now had a shoe of its own.

Her shoe!

Her missing shoe!

The one that had made her late for school and led, inadvertently, to her discovery of the Dreamffiti and the start of her incredible journey! And now, suddenly, inexplicably, here it was: her turquoise shoe, precisely where it belonged and where, seemingly, it had always been.

Suzy wished to return to Remmy and ask him how this was so, but she knew, with a sigh, that she could not. It was too late to go back. She was hurtling fast toward Reality and the bright promise of a new world.

And yet, Lucid that she was, Suzy was not without her own understanding. For as she merged into the light, a memory burst upon her, which seemed the answer to one of life's great riddles.

She was thinking, you see, of a curious blue lynx rowing down a river and singing, "*Life is but a dream...*"

"Yes," exclaimed Suzy, with a joyous laugh, "the one you wish it to be!"

THE END.

ABOUT THE AUTHOR

Brian Sanders began writing in the 2nd grade, when he scribbled out a story about a robot that could create money at the push of a button. Sadly, he hasn't been able to build a working prototype of that robot, but that hasn't stopped him from writing more stories.

After catching the screenwriting itch at Cornell University, he penned over a dozen screenplays, several of which won contests and were optioned to producers such as Multivisionnaire Pictures. He also writes short stories, a selection of which have been published in "Short Story America Volumes I & III." SNOOZY SUZY is his debut Middle Grade novel. He resides in Branchburg, NJ with his wife and two young daughters, who like to zip around on their own flying pillows.

Feel free to connect with him at briansandersbooks.com.

CPSIA information can be obtained
at www.ICGtesting.com
Printed in the USA
JSHW081034211122
33422JS00002B/6

9 780578 399539